A DEADLY CHANGE OF COURSE— OF COURSE— PLAN B

A DEADLY CHANGE
OF COURSE—
PLAN B

•

Gina Cresse

AVALON BOOKS
THOMAS BOUREGY AND COMPANY, INC.
401 LAFAYETTE STREET
NEW YORK, NEW YORK 10003

PRINTED IN THE UNITED STATES OF AMERICA
ON ACID-FREE PAPER
BY HADDON CRAFTSMEN, BLOOMSBURG, PENNSYLVANIA

Acknowledgments

I would like to thank the following people for their help and support in putting this little treasure together: My Mom and Dad, who gave me the imagination to dream. Special thanks to Dad for patiently taking a dozen calls a day to answer all my technical airplane questions—he's my own personal reference library. Doug and Arlene Richards, for their never-ending support and encouragement, and willingness to read a chapter a week (that's all I asked). Andy Folz, for his expert sailing knowledge. Kathy Holtzapple, for giving me a little insight into the Swiss Banking world. Sandy Taylor, for her keen editorial eye, and her support and encouragement (and to her husband, Ron, for painting my house). To my brother and his wife, Rick and Sue Cresse, for asking me what I was up to last Thanksgiving, which started me on a path to the next person on my list. Gary Davis, whose interest in the book gave an insecure, first-time writer much self-confidence. The list wouldn't be complete without also mentioning the rest of my family and friends, who cheered me on in this adventure—Terese, Jim, Tammy, Linda, Dolph, Jackie, Iva Lou, and Jan. Thank you all.

Chapter One

David Powers fidgeted in the hotel lobby chair as he waited for his partner, Michael Norris, to finish the checkout procedure at the front desk. It had been an exhausting trip and the two DEA agents were anxious to get home.

Working undercover in conjunction with the Mexican Judicial Police, David and Michael managed to work their way inside the finance and accounting division of the largest drug-producing operation in Mexico. Surprisingly, the administrative end of the business ran like many other legitimate Fortune 500 companies. The company, which represented itself as an agricultural farming operation, came complete with an accounting department, production and maintenance, quality control, management information systems, human resources, and even a sales and marketing division. David and Michael were introduced into the com-

1

pany as software engineers. They would be on-site for a brief two-week period to design and implement some modifications to the company's executive information systems. The two were picked for this assignment because of their extensive background in computer technology, especially network communications and software development. Once given administrative access to the network server, the pair could log into the computer from their hotel room at night and browse the entire network. Since the company strived to be a near-paperless operation, all important documents were scanned into the system and stored in various folders on-line. The network had no fire wall at all, making access to the information fairly simple. David's laptop computer was equipped with a read/write–enabled CD unit. He spent hours downloading and saving documents onto the small disks. He made it a point to make two copies of everything, just as a backup. On their last day in Mexico, he placed one of the CDs in his shirt pocket, and he packaged up the other with some souvenirs for his wife and daughter. He dropped the package, to be delivered to his home in San Diego, into the hotel lobby's mail basket.

"Hey, buddy. You ready to take your life into your own hands and chance another Mexican taxi ride to the airport?" David joked with Michael as the two picked up their bags and exited the hotel lobby.

"You bet. That's why I got into this line of work, you know. I live for the sheer thrill and excitement of third-world-country public transportation," Michael replied as he grinned with a slight cringe in his expression and waved to one of the local cabdrivers parked outside the hotel lobby.

"Great. Let's hit it. I can't wait to get home," David said as the pair loaded their bags into the trunk of the bright yellow Ford, then piled themselves into the back. Once settled in, David elbowed Michael. "Hey, buddy. Roll down your window. I swear every cab in Mexico has a major exhaust leak that pipes carbon monoxide right into the backseat."

"Is that what it is? Here all this time I thought it was the tequila making me feel so bad," Michael jested as he cranked the window handle.

Even though it was late, the airport was crowded; it seemed that everybody in the place had a need to reach out and touch someone. All the public pay phones were in use when David and Michael arrived. They sat down on some hard airport chairs, and waited for a phone to become available. Finally, the woman on the end hung up the receiver, picked up her baggage, and moved away from the booth. David jumped to his feet, and made a beeline for the vacant phone. While he waited for someone to answer his call, he checked his watch, but it had stopped. David glanced back at his partner to ask for the correct time.

Michael, oblivious to his partner's question, had that deer-caught-in-the-headlights look in his eyes. He was preoccupied watching a tall, shapely young woman walk by. She wore a fitted, cropped blazer—the deep purple color of the Mexican sky at sunset over the Pacific. She also wore a matching short skirt and high heels that accentuated her long, shapely legs. Her thick auburn hair—pulled back in a relaxed French braid—ended somewhere in the middle of her back. The beautiful natural color of her mane was even more striking set against the deep color of her suit. By the expression on his face, there could be no doubt what thoughts raced through Michael's mind.

Michael's wife had divorced him a year earlier. When

he asked her why she wanted the divorce, she told him life with him felt more like seasons of the year rather than a marriage. She said he was like spring, a season that she loved, but spring only hung around for a short while, then turned to summer, and she tired of summer. Then the fall would arrive, and bring the ever-present threat of the long, cold, lonely winter. It wasn't until David translated it for him that he understood what she said. His undercover work with the DEA would take him away for extended periods of time. In between assignments, he tried to make up for his absences by being an overly doting husband—always underfoot. She hated being left alone for such long periods of time, but he drove her nuts when he was home. After ten years of marriage, she packed her bags, and said adios. Michael took it pretty hard, and only recently began to show interest in women again.

David grinned at his partner, who nearly fell out of his chair, trying to keep the appealing young woman in his view as she disappeared around the corner.

"Hey, buddy. Am I going to have to get a leash for you before we get back to San Diego?" David asked.

"What?" Michael innocently replied, unaware that he was being observed, and even less aware of how obvious his reaction to the woman was.

Finally, David's call was answered, and he turned his attention back to the business at hand. "Hello. Victor? It's David. We're at the airport in Guadalajara. Our flight leaves in forty-five minutes."

"Great. Did you have any problems?" his superior asked.

"You kidding? Listen, we hit pay dirt here. You wouldn't believe the progress we've made with this San-chez fellow. He's not only willing to have us work with his people to shut down the Juarez Cartel operation, he says he can't do it without us. It seems we're mostly responsible for the success of the business down here.''

''What do you mean *we're* responsible?'' Victor asked.

''We were able to get copies of documents identifying major U.S. investors who've financed ninety percent of the operation. Victor, you won't believe what we've got here. I mean, there are copies of agricultural and business loan documents from Goldbank Corporation for millions of dollars. And Goldbank isn't the only one. We've got documentation implicating at least six major U.S. banks who've provided billions to finance the biggest drug operation in Mexico. And get this, Victor, there are even loans to the operation from the Mexican government. They originated from the World Bank and actually state in writing that their purpose is to promote economic development. Can you believe it? You can bet your best pony that heads are gonna roll when we get back. I think we finally have the evidence we need to shut the doors on the Juarez Cartel.''

Victor was silent for a moment. ''Victor? Are you there? Did you hear what I just told you?'' David asked excitedly, wondering if his boss had been disconnected or was just speechless.

''That's great, David. I have to admit I was skeptical when you called me last week, and said you thought you could get your hands on this information. We've been trying to deal with these people for years with no success at all. Have you got all the documentation with you?''

''Sure thing, boss. All wrapped up and sealed with a nice neat little bow,'' David said as he patted the small CD tucked safely in his pocket. ''See you in a couple of days,'' he said, then hung up the phone.

David had one more call to make before heading to the

gate. "Hello, sweetheart. It's me. I'm sorry I'm calling so late. I know I probably woke you up, but I just wanted to hear your voice."

"Oh, David. Where are you? I've been worried sick," she said as she sat up in the queen-size bed she normally shared with the man at the other end of the phone line.

"I'm still in Mexico, but I'm at the airport. I'll be home tomorrow. How are my two girls doing without me?" he asked.

"Oh, we're getting by. I just wish you were home. Emily fell off her tricycle yesterday, and scraped her elbow up a little bit. She said she wanted you to come home and kiss it better. I told her you'd get here just as soon as you could."

"That's right. I'll be home before you know it. How are you feeling? Are you getting enough rest?" he asked.

"Oh, the morning sickness is still going on, but the doctor says it'll only last a few more weeks. I sure hope so. I don't remember feeling this lousy when I was pregnant with Emily."

"Well, I'll be home soon, and I'll take care of you. I wish you would've let my mom come stay with you while I was gone. You know she'd love to help out."

"I know, but your dad is so sick, and she really needs to be with him right now. It's okay, honey. I'm getting along just fine. I'll be much better tomorrow when you walk through the front door."

"I can hardly wait to get home. I miss you so much. I'd better go now, so I don't miss my flight. Tell Emily I'll be there to kiss her elbow just as soon as I can. I love you, Amanda."

"I love you, too. Hurry home."

David walked back to the row of chairs where his partner sat. "Come on, Romeo, we've got a plane to catch."

The flight was nearly full. David and Michael squeezed their way to their seats in the back, and settled in. David noticed the woman Michael had been admiring earlier and elbowed him. "Hey, buddy. Look who just walked back into your life."

Michael's eyes lit up, and his mouth fell open, as if he were trying to say something, but couldn't get the words out.

"Mike, breathing isn't an option here. Just relax, and go introduce yourself. Don't worry. I'll save your seat for you. If she blows you out of the sky, you'll have a nice soft landing right back here next to your old buddy, David."

"You really think I should? I mean, it's only been a year since the divorce. I'm not sure I'm ready."

"You've got to be kidding. I don't think you need to worry that you're on the rebound. I mean, c'mon, guy, wake up and smell the coffee. It's been a whole year. You don't even think twice to bust down a door and nail a roomful of malicious, armed drug dealers—but put you up against a beautiful, unarmed woman and you turn into the cowardly lion."

"Who said anything about her being unarmed? She may not have a gun, but she's got enough ammunition to put me out of commission for a long time," Michael replied in self-defense.

"Come on, Mike. You don't have to go and expose your guts to her. Just make some small talk. Introduce yourself to her. What possible damage can she do to you with just your name?"

Michael thought about what his partner said; then he stood up, and stepped out into the aisle. "You're right, darn it. I'm gonna do it,'' Michael said with an initial confidence that weakened with every step as he got closer to the empty seat next to his dream woman.

Fifteen minutes had passed and Michael hadn't returned. The woman, who introduced herself as Samantha, invited him to take the seat next to her. The pair seemed to hit it off like two puppies in a pile of socks. Michael resisted the temptation to tell her all about his divorce and ex-wife—a smart move on his part. Instead, he asked her about the camera equipment she carried on board with her. Samantha explained that she was a commercial photographer and was just finishing up an assignment photographing some of Mexico's most stunning landscapes. Michael had dabbled with photography as a hobby since high school, and really enjoyed letting his creative juices flow while in the darkroom. Samantha, thrilled to have someone to talk to who shared her interest in photography, explained her techniques to Michael, who hung on every word.

It was very late, and most of the passengers on the plane slept, except of course for Michael and Samantha, who were busy planning a trip to Disneyland the following weekend. David read a magazine article about natural childbirth and practiced the breathing techniques described in the third paragraph. He glanced out the window into the moonless, pitch-black night, wondering about names for his new son or daughter.

Suddenly, the plane surged straight up like a rocket, but without the horsepower needed to propel it into space. The strong thrust woke most of the passengers from their light sleep. Then the plane banked sharply to the left. David dropped his magazine, and tried to shelter his head from the items falling out of the overhead storage compartments. Passengers who weren't seat-belted flew across the aisle onto the other passengers. He looked across the aisle at the mother and little boy in the seats opposite his. Terror shone in the little boy's face as he cried and begged his mother to make it stop. She held him tight against her and told him not to worry—it would be all right.

Sheer panic raced through the plane as it continued to roll onto its back and then dive sharply downward toward the earth. People were screaming hysterically and praying loudly for the grace of God to save them from this nightmare ride.

Samantha buried her face into Michael's chest as he squeezed her, trying to calm her fears.

David's life flashed before his eyes. He remembered his college graduation—seeing how proud his father was of him for graduating top of his class. He saw every detail of his wedding—the beautiful bride walking down the long aisle of the church on her father's arm. He remembered the day Emily, his little baby girl, was born and how elated and scared he was at the thought of being a father. His last thought was of Amanda and Emily and the new baby on the way, and how they would make it without him there to take care of them.

David spoke the words, "Please, dear God . . ." just as Flight 9602 crashed into the side of a mountain, exploding into a huge mass of flames and smoke. Burning debris flew for miles. Heat from the plane's nearly full fuel tanks was so intense that trees within a quarter-mile radius of the crash site were ignited. There could be no survivors.

Chapter Two

The alarm clock startled me like a sudden, unexpected gunshot on a quiet afternoon. I rolled over in my bunk to look at the time. It was five in the morning. I had to think for a moment why I was getting up so early. Was it a mistake? For the life of me, I couldn't remember why I set the alarm. I lay there for several minutes, and felt the swaying of my bed as the wake of an early morning fisherman's boat lapped at the sides of my cozy home—the *Plan B.* Slowly, consciousness brought me out of a recently recurring dream—the one where I'm married to Mel Gibson—and hurled me into the reality of my rather uneventful life. I remembered something about having to be at a particular place early this morning, but where? Oh yes, the auction. My friend Jason told me if I could get there as soon as the

10

gates opened, I might beat out a lot of the competition, and make some pretty good deals.

My name is Devonie Lace. I'm a thirty-six-year-old self-employed treasure hunter. I was a senior database administrator for a major communications company for thirteen years. On my thirty-fourth birthday, the database went down, and it stayed down. It took eleven days, at a cost of over one million dollars per day, to recover. I lost nine pounds in that eleven-day period. I also lost half my hair—the half that hadn't turned gray yet. For my thirty-fifth birthday, I had a minor heart attack.

When I got out of the hospital, I quit my job, sold my house, and bought a nice little thirty-five-foot sailboat. She's a 1969 Coronado sloop with a ten-foot beam and a fiberglass hull. She has a beautiful, meticulously maintained teak deck. Originally, she had a single gasoline engine, but the previous owner felt safer with diesel, so he replaced it. I affectionately named her *Plan B*. Plan A had been to somehow become the most successful, highest-paid database administrator the world had ever seen. Unfortunately, the price was too high.

As soon as she arrived from her previous home in San Francisco, I had a new sail custom-made for her. I designed it myself, inspired by the exquisite Pacific sunsets that bless this side of the country like a daily gift from heaven. The base of the sail is a beautiful deep sapphire blue, that gradually lightens to a nearly transparent azure at the top. In the center is a bright yellow orb with various shades of red, orange, and white sunbeams shooting out in all directions. In front of the sun is the silhouette of a graceful seabird gliding effortlessly on the winds of the sea. I sketched the design one evening while sitting on the beach. While I sat, enjoying the feeling of the warm sand between my toes, I contemplated how I could change the world. I had just gotten out of the hospital and was taking a short doctor-ordered vacation before returning to work. It finally dawned on me that I probably couldn't change *the* world, but I could certainly change *my* world. That was the day before I made the call to my boss, letting her know I wouldn't be returning to work.

So, now I live on my beautiful little boat in a peaceful marina near San Diego. I haven't mastered the art of sailing, yet. My first venture out of the marina cost me about four thousand dollars. I really thought this boat could turn a lot sharper and faster than it does. The man in the slip next to mine will attest to the fact that you can't decide, at the last minute, to park your thirty-five-foot sailboat instead of taking one more practice run around the harbor. Although the damage seemed very minor to me, repairs to yachts are somehow equivalent to repairs on, say, a Mercedes, Porsche, or Rolls-Royce. I promised the owner of the marina I will not venture out of my slip unassisted again until I have completed the boating and sailing course the Coast Guard offers for a reasonable fee—I believe it's free.

Although I do own the *Plan B* outright, there is still the matter of monthly slip fees, boat bottom cleaning, annual boat painting, personal property taxes, insurance, fuel for my Jeep, food, and all the other little necessities of life that require some sort of monthly income. To accommodate this unfortunate requirement, I perform a plethora of income-earning activities. On Friday and Saturday nights, I'm a cocktail waitress at King Rooster's Bar & Grille—a restaurant in the marina where I live. The work is mindless and sometimes demeaning, but the tips are great, and it's really the only steady, reliable income I have at the moment. The rest of the time, I read the legal sections of our local newspaper looking for probate sales, foreclosure sales, and auctions. I don't have a lot of capital to invest in anything big, but once in a while, I can pick up some interesting small items—like jewelry and watches—and resell them for a profit. Lately, I've become interested in a particular kind of auction, the kind I plan to attend today.

We Americans are a funny lot. When I was a little girl, I don't remember ever seeing a self-storage complex. What did people do with all their stuff back then? Did they throw it away when they didn't have room for it anymore? Maybe they kept all the stuff they owned in their house or garage until they died, and left the disposal of the valuables to the survivors. Today, it seems everyone has more stuff than they have room. Why? What has changed in the last thirty years? I counted fifty self-storage complexes in the phone book just in my little community alone. Maybe a lot of people live on their boats like me, but don't want to give up their washers, dryers, and sofas in case they decide that boat living isn't really for them. I don't know for sure, but I do know that when people fail to pay their storage rent, eventually the owners of the complexes auction the contents of the units to help offset their losses. I have been to several of these auctions, and I really enjoy the anticipation of buying something valuable for next to nothing. It's like a treasure hunt. Sometimes you end up with an empty cardboard box, but there's always the chance you might wind up with a chest of gold.

Mostly, I wind up with semiuseful appliances that I can resell through my friend Jason, who owns a small used-appliance sales and repair shop downtown. He's the one who clued me in on today's auction. Apparently, there was a misprint in the paper that announced this auction. It actually starts one hour earlier than was stated in the ad. They don't really let you inspect the contents of the units very well before you bid on them, so it's kind of a gamble when you lay out hard cash for something unknown. The less competition in bidding, the better for me, since I'm no longer bringing home that substantial annual salary that I had become accustomed to—in my prior life.

I rolled out of my bunk, and staggered to the bathroom. Oh, I mean "head." Boats don't have bathrooms, as my neighbor informed me, which is where he was when I accidentally parked my boat in his slip. I don't think park is the correct term, either. I think dock is the word I should use. I have a lot to learn about this boat business. I do know the things that look like ropes are not ropes, but are actually lines. They sure look like ropes, but each time I use the term, I get a funny look and a correction from whichever expert is helping me out that day. I do appreciate the assistance I get from the local sailors. If it weren't for them, I'd never get to sail outside of my slip. But they are all so picky about using the right words for things. Non-technical terms like "thingamabob" and "doohickey" go right over their heads. They are really nice people, but I would have to say for the most part, they are technical-term snobs.

I fixed myself the usual low-fat, low-sugar, low-taste breakfast, and turned on the radio. It was August, and, although the air was foggy, the day was going to be a bright and beautiful seventy-five degrees. I love the weather here. It beats the heck out of the summers in the valley I came from, where summertime temperatures can regularly exceed one hundred degrees.

After breakfast, I fed Marty, my pet goldfish. Actually,

he's Marty number four. I don't think I have this goldfish business down to a science yet, either. They keep going belly-up on me. If this Marty doesn't survive, I'm switching to some other kind of fish. Jason suggested some type of plastic fish substitute—a faux fish, I believe is the term he used. He said it would be more humane than subjecting another poor living creature to my apparent lack of skill in fish ownership. He could be right. Personally, I think the lady at the pet shop, where I buy my Martys, is selling me defective fish. I believe she is doing this to encourage me to buy a more expensive type of animal, like a parrot.

I showered, and dressed in my most professional attire— a pair of white shorts, an oversize red-and-white striped T-shirt, and deck shoes. I put on a jacket to fend off the morning chill. If nothing else, I have perfected the sailing wardrobe, and certainly look like I should know what I'm doing. I checked my watch; it was six-thirty. (I should mention that I move slowly in the morning; most people don't require ninety minutes to get ready, even for their own wedding.)

"See ya later, Marty," I said as I stepped through the hatch onto the deck, turning back to lock the *Plan B*. I gingerly hopped off of my beautiful boat onto the dock, and quickly headed toward my Jeep in the marina parking area.

"Good morning, Mr. Cartwright," I called to my neighbor, who was out polishing some piece of chrome on his yacht. I've often been tempted to ask him how Little Joe and Hoss are, but after the parking incident, I don't think he'd appreciate my sense of humor. I think I'd better wait until he really gets to know and love me, before I start kidding around with him.

"Good morning, Miss Lace. Early day for you, isn't it?" He seemed surprised to see me out and about at this hour.

"Yes. I have some business this morning. I hope it turns out successful for me. I could use the extra money for those sailing lessons I've been wanting to take," I said, grinning. I watched his expression for a reaction. Yes, there was a smile. I think I may *finally* be getting to him.

I walked quickly, past some of my neighbors' slips. Most of the boats here in the marina are weekend toys. Only a few of us actually live on our boats. I could hear Mr. Rowden banging some pots and pans inside his ill-kept fishing boat, *Voluntary Solitary.* He spends most of his time out fishing. He must be having some mechanical problems. I haven't seen him spend this many days in a row tied up to the dock since he had to have his engines rebuilt last season.

Chapter Three

Jason, already at A-1 Mini Storage when I arrived, waved as I pulled into the parking lot. The manager was just unlocking the office as I parked my Jeep in the small lot outside the chain-link fence. This complex seemed to have many more security features than others I've seen. The rates are higher too—I guess to cover the extra costs for twenty-four-hour security guards and surveillance cameras.

"Good morning, Devonie. I wasn't sure if you'd be able to drag yourself out of bed this early in the morning," Jason said with a smile smeared on his face.

"Oh, come on, Jason. You know I used to get up at five A.M. every day when I was part of the rat race. I can get up with the rest of the early birds—if I have to," I defended.

"Come on in, folks," said the man with the keys. "You're an eager bunch, aren't you?"

There were about a dozen anxious people waiting with

17

us outside the doors. We filed in, and followed the manager into the office.

"Okay, folks. We're gonna get started on time this morning. Let me get my clipboard here, and we'll head out. I'm gonna open up the units being offered today. You all can look inside, but you need to stay behind the markers we've placed in front of the doors. I'm gonna give you each a map showing the particular units we're auctioning today. The preview period will last for about an hour, then the bidding will begin. We'll start at this end of the complex, and work our way down each row until we get to the end. As you can see, we're looking at about twenty units. Some of the smaller ones have been combined with others into single lots, so be aware when you're bidding," the manager announced as he pulled a clipboard from the wall, and began flipping through pages.

He handed each of us a photocopy map of the complex. They each had twenty yellow Xs marked on them. I kept looking for the *You Are Here* X, so I could put the thing in perspective. I forgot to mention, I'm directionally challenged. I don't have an internal compass like a lot of people do. I'm so glad I live at the ocean now, so at least I can almost always tell which way is west.

I followed Jason out the door. "Hey, Jason. How do you read this thing?" I asked as I hurried to keep pace with him.

"You're kidding. Right?"

"Yeah. I'm kidding. I mean, it's so obvious. But, just exactly where are we, say, in relation to this yellow X, here?" I asked with a slightly helpless tone in my voice as I arbitrarily pointed to a mark on the map.

"Devonie, how in the world did you ever manage to

program a computer?'' Jason asked as he stopped and pointed out where we were on the map.

"Easy, Jason. You don't need to know the difference between east and west when you're writing an application to pay bills or track inventory. Besides, I wasn't a computer programmer, I was a database administrator,'' I replied indignantly.

"I'm sorry, Devonie, I didn't mean that the way it sounded.''

"That's okay, Jason. Little comments like that reconfirm my belief that I'm making the right decision to stay single the rest of my life.''

"Come on, Devonie. You know you don't want to be alone the rest of your life. Don't you ever wish for a little romance? Everyone's got to have someone. Where would Romeo be without Juliet?''

"Alive,'' I answered.

"Very funny. If you'd just give some poor guy a chance, you'd see that all men aren't jerks.''

"Like who?''

"Like me, Devonie Lace.''

Oh, great. This is not a direction I want to go. We have had this conversation a dozen times, and he still doesn't get it. I have come to cherish my freedom and independence, and am not anxious to mess it up by introducing a significant other into my life. Marty, the goldfish, is as much commitment as I care to make at this point. Years ago, I made the foolish mistake of letting someone get too close. I put all my faith and trust in him, and he let me down. Now, I find it much safer to keep everyone at arm's length, at least emotionally. This way, I can't get hurt, although it does get a little lonely sometimes. "Jason, we've been over this. I'm not going to discuss it again. Just tell me where these little units are; I don't want to bid on any big stuff today.''

''Fine, Dev. Have it your way. You just head down this row and around the corner to the right. All the small units are on the far end down there,'' he said as he pointed down the long row of steel roll-up doors. ''Want me to walk you over there, so you don't get lost?'' he asked. The sarcasm in his voice poisoned his response.

''No, thanks. I can handle it,'' I said as I started to walk off. ''Oh, and by the way, Jason, what you just said about not being a jerk? You sure could have fooled me.''

The man with the keys opened the six small units being auctioned off. Four of them were combined into two separate lots, and the other two were being sold as individual units. I peered into the first one on the end—nothing but cardboard boxes with no labels or markings at all. They could have been full of old clothes and a bunch of worthless junk. On the other hand, they could have been full of priceless treasures. You just couldn't tell. About seven months ago, I passed up bidding on a unit that looked worthless. As it turned out, the unit contained a rare coin collection that proved to be worth thousands of dollars. The delinquent tenants of the unit didn't realize the value of what they had.

The next pair of open doors revealed a little more information. Again, they were full of cardboard boxes, but at least these were labeled. Some were marked TAXES with the year designated. Some were marked OLD COLLEGE TEXTBOOKS, and another was marked DIVORCE PAPERS. It was easy to see why someone would let this storage unit go, especially if finances were bad enough to quit paying some bills. I decided not to bid on this one.

The last unit held the most promise of all. There were two small safes, three briefcases, a small file cabinet, and what looked like a laptop computer in a black carrying case. There was a second case—probably a bubble jet printer—but my view was partially blocked, and I couldn't see the whole thing. The rest of the crowd headed down the row toward my claim. I wished I could quickly shut the door until they passed. It was obvious this unit contained at least something of value.

"Oh, look, Beth, I think that's a computer in that case there," a man said to his wife as he pointed at *my* find.

"No way, Tom. You've already got two of those darn things, and I can't even get you away from them long enough to help me around the house. I've already told you, we're bidding on that unit with the nice Sears Kenmore washer and dryer set. Now, come on."

"Yep. Tom is whipped," I whispered to myself as Beth pulled the reluctant Tom by the arm away from the unit.

Another man, in a light green shirt and pastel-colored plaid shorts, was eyeing my goods with a covetous look about him. He appeared to be in his mid-forties, with a bit of a beer belly, and a thinning hairline that was just starting to show gray at the temples. His mustache was more gray than the hair on his head, and it was trimmed sort of crooked on one side. He wore a red fanny pack that was adjusted too loosely. From the back, he reminded me of one of those monkeys with the bright red bottoms during mating season. He turned to me, and said, "Looks like one of those laptop computers in there, huh?"

"Oh, I don't think so. It's probably just the case. Why would anyone store a computer like that? They would be using it too often to keep it in storage. Don't you think?"

He smiled, and scratched his head. "You're probably

right. I wonder what's in those safes?'' he said as he leaned over to get a better look.

I could tell this was going to be a problem. I decided the best action to take now was to seem uninterested. I walked over to the first unit, and studied the boxes—like a sports fan stands in front of the rows and rows of television sets in a department store, watching the same game on twelve TVs. Four more people were drooling over my unit full of treasures, and I didn't like it at all. I checked my watch. The bidding would be starting in about fifteen minutes. They probably wouldn't get to this unit for about thirty minutes after that. I started calculating exactly how much I could afford to bid. I decided to take a look at the rest of the lots before the bidding started.

Jason was camped out at the Kenmore washer and dryer unit. Little did Tom and Beth realize that Jason would give them a run for their money. I've seen that look in Jason's eye before. He wanted that pair of appliances, and nothing was going to keep him from having them.

By the time the auctioneer got to my unit, there were at least twenty people gathered around the door. I set myself up as close to the center front as possible.

''Okay. This looks like a pretty promising lot here. Let's start the bidding at five hundred,'' the auctioneer called.

Five hundred dollars? Was he kidding? I looked around at the rest of the faces. No one was jumping.

''Fifty dollars!'' I called out bravely.

''You've got to be kidding, lady. Just one of those safes is worth five times that amount,'' he answered back.

''Do you have a hold on this lot, mister?'' I asked him confidently.

''No, ma'am.''

"Then fifty dollars is my bid."

He gave me a distressed look, then returned to the business at hand.

"I have fifty! Do I hear seventy-five?" he yelled out to the crowd.

"Fifty-five!" I heard from somewhere behind me. It was Tom. Then I saw Beth punch him in the arm.

"Ouch! What'd you do that for?" he cried out innocently.

"You know darn well what for," I heard her reply.

"Sixty!" I countered.

"One hundred!" came from the man in the green shirt. I could see trouble on the way. I could not afford to spend more than two hundred and fifty dollars today, or I would be fishing for my dinner for the rest of the month. I wondered what Marty would taste like with tartar sauce and French fries.

"One hundred and one!" I called out.

The small, vertical crease in the auctioneer's forehead deepened as he glared at me through two squinting eyes. His irritation with me was hard to hide. "Lady. Just so we're not here all day, why don't we try to keep this to—"

"Is there a rule that says I have to bid in certain increments?" I asked defiantly.

He gave me a look that would make a junkyard dog turn tail and run. "I have one hundred and one. Do I hear one hundred and ten?"

"One hundred and fifty!"

Oh, great. This was a third bidder I had never seen before. I was beginning to sweat, and I wondered if I had remembered to put my deodorant on this morning.

"One hundred and fifty-one!" I called out.

There was that look again. I smiled and batted my big

blue eyes at the auctioneer, but he didn't seem to be amused.

There was a slight pause. For a moment, I thought I had done it. Then, from the man in the green, came a loud and definite, "Two hundred dollars!"

Before I could get my two hundred and one out, the third bidder spoke up. "Two fifty!"

I looked at him with an injured expression, and raised my hand. "Two hundred and fifty-one!" Rats! What was I doing? I stepped over my limit. I couldn't lose control, not now. It was time to back out, and let the other two bidders duke it out.

The green shirt bid two seventy-five, and it looked like he was going to get it. There was silence for a moment.

"I have two hundred and seventy-five dollars. Do I hear three hundred?"

I looked at the man in green. He smiled smugly at me with that crooked mustache, as if he had just beaten a politician at a game of liar's poker. I raised my hand with determination, and called out, "Three hundred dollars!"

The auctioneer was growing impatient. "I have three hundred going once, going twice. Sold to the little lady in the front for three hundred dollars. You can pay in the main office. When we're done with all the lots, you can bring your vehicle in here, and load it up."

Wonderful, except that I was fifty dollars shy of my bid. Where was I going to get the extra cash to pay for this?

"Hey, Dev. Congratulations," a voice from behind me said.

"Jason. Thanks. Want to buy a safe for fifty bucks?"

"You need fifty dollars to cover your bid?"

"How'd you guess?"

"I know you too well, Devonie. Sure, I'll give you fifty bucks—but not for a safe. I'll take that computer, though."

"Are you kidding? You'd rather spend fifty on what's probably some old 286 dog of a computer—if there's a computer in there at all? Think about it, Jason. There must be something pretty valuable in there if it's important enough to lock up in a safe."

"You want the computer, don't you?"

"Yeah. I do. I could keep my records on it instead of in that crazy notebook I have to deal with. Besides, you've already got a nice Pentium desktop PC."

"Okay. I'll take that safe there in the front, the one with the eagle picture on the door. Here's the money," Jason said as he handed me two twenties and a ten.

"Thanks, Jason. I take back what I said about you being a jerk."

"Anytime, Dev. You know I'd do anything for you, like the fool that I am."

"Did you get your washer and dryer?"

"Yeah, but you wouldn't believe what I had to give for it. Some crazy lady kept bidding against me. She just wouldn't let it go—sort of like a female pit bull. I wanted to muzzle her."

Visions of Beth and Jason duking it out over a washer and dryer amused me for a brief moment.

"I'll help you load your stuff in your van if you'll help me with this stuff."

"Sure thing, Dev, but they won't be done for a while. Want to go have a hot chocolate or something while we wait?"

"Sure. Just let me go pay for my treasures, and I'll meet you in the coffee shop. Oh, can I keep this stuff in your warehouse? No room on the boat, you know."

"Yeah, but I'm going to have to charge you storage."

"Storage? How much?" I asked.

"I'm just kidding, Dev. Jeez. Can't you even take a joke?"

The safes were heavier than I expected. The two of us struggled to get them in the back of my Jeep. "I'll have to get a locksmith to open these for me," I said.

"I have a friend who can open them. He's one of San Diego's finest, but in his spare time, he likes to fool around with locks and stuff. His grandfather was a locksmith—taught him everything he knows. He's out of town today, but first thing in the morning, I'll give him a call."

"Great. I think I'll take those briefcases home with me. I bet I can pick the locks on them. If I can't, I'll bring them over, and see if your friend can open them, too."

"Sure thing. Let's get this stuff over to the shop. I've got to open up for business before I lose all my customers."

We unloaded everything in the warehouse behind Jason's shop—where he stores all kinds of parts and machines that he's working on. I have a small corner marked off with tape on the floor. This is where I keep most of the larger items—the ones I haven't sold yet. Also, I've stored just a few things I couldn't part with when I sold my house. A cedar chest my grandma had given me when I was a little girl is stored here. It has become affectionately known as my "hopeless" chest. We placed the locked file cabinet next to it. My safe sat next to the chest, and if I brought any more in here, I'd have to move the tape to give myself more real estate.

I unzipped the case around the laptop. Pay dirt. It was a Gateway Pentium laptop. Those things sell for around five thousand bucks. I tried to power it up, but the battery was dead. No surprise. No telling how long it had been sitting in that storage unit. I rummaged through the case. There was no electrical cord, but there was a CD-ROM unit. I put it in the front seat of the Jeep with the briefcases.

"Thanks for all your help, Jason," I said. "I'm going to get this stuff over to the boat. I've got to work for Carla at the Grille tonight. She's got some party or something she has to go to, so I said I'd cover for her today."

"Okay. I'll give you a call in the morning after I get a hold of my friend, Mark. I can hardly wait to see what's in there."

"I know. Isn't it exciting? I just love this business."

I carried the computer and printer down the dock on my first trip. Mr. Cartwright was polishing some brass now. "Afternoon, Miss Lace. Successful day, I hope?" he inquired.

"It surely was, Mr. Cartwright. A great day."

I unlocked the hatch door and stepped down into my little galley. I set the cases on the table, and glanced over at Marty's bowl. "Darn," I said aloud. There he was, belly-up, like a lazy cat on a hot summer day. "That's it. I give up."

I gave him a brief burial at sea and washed out the fish-bowl. No more pets—I just can't take it.

I brought the briefcases to the boat, and got ready for work. I was going to be late if I didn't get going soon. I'd have to try to open the cases after I got home. I locked the boat up, and jogged down the dock to the Grille. All I could think about was what could be in those cases.

Chapter Four

It was just past midnight when I finally finished up at the Grille, and I was beat. The place was much busier than usual. I spent the whole shift racing from table to table, then back to the bar. The clientele were more demanding than usual—I bit my tongue on several occasions to keep from giving some rude drunk a piece of my mind. I've learned that the ill-mannered ones tend to be the best tippers; I guess it eases their consciences. I really wasn't cut out for this kind of work, but I can put up with almost any idiot, if I know I have to, in order to pay my slip rent that month. I staggered down the dock to my boat. I had been up since five in the morning.

I removed a collection of small tools from my purse. Gary, the bartender from the Grille, gave them to me earlier, along with some brief instruction on the fine art of lock-picking. I practiced on an olive and a maraschino cherry. Somehow, I don't think it's quite the same as a real lock. I sat down with the first case—a very nice brown leather job with the initials *RAK* embossed on the side. I played with the lock for ten minutes, with no luck. I grew tired and impatient. I set the case down, and went below to get into my toolbox. I returned with the Wonder Bar, strategically placed it under the latch of the locked case, and gave it a good yank. Bingo. The container was unlocked—and now, completely useless as a briefcase.

I lifted the lid of the case. My mouth fell open, and I began to hyperventilate. I expected to find business papers, brochures, and if I was lucky, a cellular phone or a really nice calculator. What I didn't expect to find was cash— lots of cash. Row after row of bundled hundred-dollar bills. My knees went weak and I collapsed in the chair.

"Wow. How much money is that?" I said aloud. I couldn't bring myself to touch it. I just stared in amazement. Why would someone put that much money in a self-storage unit? And why, for heaven's sake, would they let it be auctioned off for lack of payment? Slowly, I reached for the case, and picked up one of the bundles. I started counting. I had to start over four times. I finally concluded that the bundle contained five hundred bills, each of them being of the one-hundred-dollar denomination. That one bundle amounted to fifty thousand dollars. I looked back at the case. There were nine more bundles identical to this one. My heart raced, and I felt faint. That's a half-million dollars sitting there on my kitchen table. I pinched myself and started looking around for Mel Gibson—this had to be a dream.

"Okay. Calm down, Devonie," I told myself. I got my breathing under control, and replaced the bundle of bills. I checked the pockets in the lid of the case. I found something tucked in the pouch—a year-old airline ticket to Geneva. The storage unit account had to be delinquent for at least a year before they would auction it off—according to the manager of the complex. Whomever the money belonged to must have come to some horrible demise at about the time this ticket was purchased. No one still breathing would let a half-million dollars go. Maybe the person was in prison, and couldn't get to the money before he was incarcerated. No. He would have arranged for someone to get the money before he'd lose it. He must have been dead—that was the only logical explanation.

I checked the pockets for more information. I found a passport for a Robert Allen Kephart. He appeared in the photo to be in his mid-forties, and a knockout. His sandy blond hair and mustache complemented a pair of deep hazel-blue eyes. He had that Robert Redford look—the rugged outdoorsy type. I removed the only other thing I could find in the case—a small notepad. I tried to decipher a name scribbled on the first page, but the writing proved to be illegible. It looked like Carl Hobbs or Hebbs, but I couldn't be sure. Below that, in clear print, the words PAID IN FULL were underlined in bold ink. A hundred scenarios passed through my mind as to where this money came from, and none of them even slightly resembled anything legal. I doubted this was anyone's bingo winnings, or the proceeds from the sale of a car. I glanced suspiciously at the other two briefcases—afraid to think what might be in them.

I didn't even bother trying to pick the lock on the next case; I just applied the Wonder Bar, and opened it. Any slight hope I might have had, that this money was not part of some illegal activity, was shattered when I lifted the lid. This case was specifically designed to hold a gun, a very large gun, with several attachments. I'm not familiar with firearms, or their related paraphernalia, but from what I've seen in the movies, I was looking at a pretty high-tech scope and a silencer. Also in the case, I found ammunition and a pair of gloves.

What have I gotten myself into? I thought. I had a feeling life, as I knew it, would not be the same after today.

The third case was not locked. It contained a toothbrush, toothpaste, dental floss, a shaving kit, a new light blue polo shirt, and a clean pair of underwear. I found a small address book tucked into the side pocket. The book, like new, contained only one entry—Kerstin Weibel. Her address was in Geneva. Next to her name was a number, in a strange format. It must be a European phone number, I thought. Inside the front cover were two sets of numbers penciled in: 10:42:58 and 11:29:47. I stared at the page for a minute, and processed the information before my eyes. I reached for my phone, and dialed.

"Hello. Jason?"

"Devonie? Is that you? Why are you calling me at . . . What time is it anyway? For Pete's sake, it's two A.M. What's going on?"

"Jason. Don't call your friend to open those safes this morning. I think I found the combinations in one of these briefcases," I rattled on, my voice quavering.

"You called and woke me up at two in the morning to tell me that? What's going on, Dev?"

"I can't tell you now. Just don't tell anyone about those safes—or anything else I picked up at the auction today. Do you hear me, Jason? Are you awake enough to understand what I'm telling you?"

"Yeah, Dev. I hear you. What'd you find in those cases, anyway? Secret spy stuff or something?"

"You wouldn't believe me if I told you. For now, I'm

going to keep it under my hat—at least until I figure it out. My senses tell me things might get a little tense, and the fewer people who know about what I found today, the better.''

''That's it, Dev; I'm coming over. You're in some sort of trouble,'' Jason said, in the most gallant voice he could muster—at this hour.

''No, Jason. Right now, I'm going to try to get some sleep. First thing in the morning, I'm going to take care of some business. After that, I'll come over to the warehouse, and we can try to open the safes, and the file cabinet. Don't worry about me. I'm fine.''

''How do you know you're fine, Dev?''

''Because if anyone else knew about what was in that storage unit today, they would have outbid me, for sure. No. I'm pretty certain that I'm the only one who knows what was in that unit—but I'm also pretty sure that someone will be looking for it.''

''What is *it,* Dev?'' he asked.

''I can't tell you right now, Jason. Just don't call your friend, and don't tell anyone about this. Okay? I'll see you in the morning. Go back to sleep. 'Bye.''

I tore the two relevant pages from the address book, and slipped them into my purse. I replaced the address book, and closed the case. I put all three cases in my closet, and shut the door. For the first time since I bought the boat, it occurred to me that I don't have a very secure place to lock anything up. I slipped out of my clothes, and into a large, oversize T-shirt. I lay in bed for what seemed like hours, but when I looked at the clock, only ten minutes had passed. I heard footsteps on the dock, and voices just outside my boat. My heart began racing again. I held my breath. The voices stopped—then I heard laughter. Just a couple of fishermen out for an early start. Relieved, I slowly let out my breath and closed my eyes. I needed to relax and get some sleep, so I could think straight. At some point, exhaustion finally took over, and I fell asleep.

As daylight peeked through my easterly porthole, I reluctantly woke from another dream. This time, the sweet aroma of Mel's café mocha, and the mouthwatering taste of his ham, cheese, and avocado omelet mingled with the usual smells of morning sea air. That Mel, he's such a sweetheart.

Chapter Five

I secured the two cases closed with some duct tape I managed to scrounge from my tool kit. I have come to believe you can fix almost anything if you have duct tape, electrical ties, bungee cords, and Supergrip. My number-one priority would be to get that money to a secure place. I rented a larger safe-deposit box at my bank, and tucked it away for safekeeping. I wanted to know more about the gun before I made any plans for it.

My friend, Joe, runs a pawnshop in town. He has sort of taken me under his wing, and makes it a point to watch out for me. When I first came to San Diego, I had been cheated by some pretty unscrupulous dealers. They convinced me the items I had to sell were basically worthless, and offered to take them off my hands for next to nothing—just to save me a trip to the dump. Then one day, I met a man in the Grille, who was wearing one of the unique watches I had practically given away to a pawnbroker. He was only too happy to brag about the newly purchased item on his wrist—bought for a mere six hundred dollars. Heaven knows, it was worth twice that much, but he was such a great wheeler-dealer, he talked the shop owner down to his price.

Jason introduced me to Joe. He cringed at some of my horror stories. The actions of his lowlife peers appalled him. Joe has always been honest with me. Sometimes, he lets me sell things on consignment. He has gotten me some very good prices for many of the items I've picked up. He knows a lot of people—people who deal in all sorts of things. I knew if he couldn't tell me anything about the gun, he would know someone who could.

"Hey, Joe. How's business?" I asked as I stepped into his shop.

"Devonie. Good to see you," he said as he gave me a big bear hug, and a kiss on the cheek. "Business is good. In fact, I just sold that nice ruby and diamond ring you brought in here last month. I have a check for you in my office. A real nice young couple came in yesterday morning. They're getting married, and wanted something unique—quality, but couldn't afford the Hope Diamond. You know how it is."

"Yeah. I know how it is, Joe. How's Sarah doing?" I asked.

"Oh. She's just fine. She's on some new health-craze kick now. Gonna sell vitamins and minerals, or something. All I know is, it's gonna cost me a fortune to get her started. I'm gonna have to expand my business, just to support hers."

"Vitamins and minerals? Why don't you have her send me a brochure. I'll be her first customer."

"Sure thing, Dev. What've you got in the case there?"

Joe asked, pointing to my very nice briefcase, strapped with six feet of duct tape.

"Well, Joe. It's something I picked up at that self-storage auction yesterday. It kind of threw me for a loop. Do you know anything about guns?"

"Guns? Well, I know a little. I know I can't sell them. I don't have a license."

"I'm not interested in selling it, at least not yet. I just want to find out more about this particular one," I said as I peeled off the duct tape.

A customer came in the door to look around. I quickly retaped the case closed. "Can I show this to you in your office?" I asked Joe, uneasy about letting any strangers know what I had.

"Sure. I'll get Margo to watch the counter. Go on back. I'll be right there."

I held the case under my arm, and made my way back to Joe's office. I set the case on his desk, and peeled the tape off again. After a few minutes, Joe came through the door.

"Let's take a look at what you've got here," he said as I lifted the lid. Joe's eyes widened and he took a full step back. "Oh my. You weren't kidding. That's some gun."

"Can you tell me anything about it?"

Joe picked up the weapon, and checked to be sure it wasn't loaded. "You know, this looks like a serious setup here—I mean with the scope and the silencer and all. I have a friend who knows everything there is to know about this sort of thing. He has an office downtown. I could call him up, and ask him to come take a look. Would that be okay? He could probably give you a pretty accurate appraisal."

"Do you know him very well, Joe? I'd like to keep this under my hat. I'm a little nervous about having it."

"Oh, sure. You can trust old Tony. He and I go way back. We were in the war together—he saved my skin more than once."

"Okay. Let's give him a call. I'm really curious about this thing." The lack of enthusiasm in my voice tipped Joe off to my uneasiness.

Tony Marino—a tall, slender man with salt-and-pepper hair and a meticulously groomed mustache—arrived shortly after Joe called him. He wore a very expensive Italian suit, and the sharpest shoes I've ever seen on a man. I admired his taste in clothes.

"How are you doing, Tony?" Joe greeted as he held out a hand to his friend.

"What's this handshake business, old buddy?" Tony asked, as he wrapped his arms around his friend, and gave him a hug and patted him firmly on the back. "I'm just dandy, you old codger. When are you and Sarah going to invite me over for dinner? It's been too long since we've gotten together, and told all those exaggerated war stories. Every time we tell them, they get more exciting and death-defying."

"How about Saturday night? I'm sure Sarah has something she'll want to show you," Joe said, giving me a wink. "Tony, I'd like you to meet a friend of mine. This is Miss Devonie Lace."

Tony held out his hand. "Very pleased to meet you, Miss Lace."

"Same here," I said as I shook his hand with my usual gentle-but-firm handshake. It's one that I have worked to perfect over the years. If I have been successful, it relays the message, "Hi. I'm Devonie Lace. I may look helpless and naive, but I'm not—so don't mess with me."

"Joe. You never told me you had such beautiful young

women friends. Will Devonie be joining us for dinner on Saturday?''

''Now, you just watch your step there, Tony. Devonie here is young enough to be your daughter,'' Joe warned his friend, as if he were my father.

It's always nice to get a compliment. I smiled and graciously accepted his charming comment.

''Actually, Tony, we have some serious business here. We need your expert opinion on something. Take a look at this,'' Joe said as he opened the case.

''Well, what have we got here? This is a nine-millimeter Spectre, very lethal weapon. Is this yours, Devonie?'' Tony asked.

''Well, yes. I seem to have acquired it quite by accident. I would like to know a little more about it—if you think you can help me.''

Tony picked up and inspected each piece carefully. He was quiet for a long time. Then he looked at me, and asked, ''Does anyone else know you have this?''

''No. Just you and Joe,'' I answered.

''May I ask how you came to acquire it?''

''I picked it up—'' I stopped. I really didn't know this man well enough to trust him. I wondered how much I should tell him. ''It's not important how I got it. Is it?''

''Miss Lace. This is a nine-millimeter Spectre, equipped with a nine-inch barrel for superior accuracy. It's an extremely lethal weapon. It's the same kind the Italian Police Special Operations Unit uses.''

Then he picked up the scope, and turned it in his hands a couple of times. ''This is a laser sighting scope. It shoots a laser beam at your target, and tells you exactly where your bullet will hit—and I mean exactly. And finally, this is a silencer—an EM-F2, if I'm not mistaken—designed to make the firing as quiet as possible.''

Tony gave me a very serious look, as if he were a doctor telling me that I had an untreatable case of cancer, and only a short time to live. ''In my opinion, the only kind of people who would use a setup like this would be hired killers. Those kind of people don't generally leave their tools of the trade lying around, for just anyone to pick up. I would guess that somewhere, someone is looking for this. The kind of people I'm talking about would stop at nothing to get back something they've lost. Do you understand what I'm telling you, Miss Lace?''

I swallowed hard, and shook my head affirmatively. I knew exactly what he was talking about. ''I think I'll just put this thing in a safe place, for now, and not tell anyone about it. I'm sure I can trust the two of you to keep my secret, until I decide what to do with it?''

''Of course, you can trust me,'' Joe said.

''That's a wise decision, Devonie. I could probably find a buyer for it, if you were so inclined. I mean, if you want to get it off your hands,'' Tony offered.

''I'll keep that in mind, but for the moment, I would prefer we keep this just between the three of us.''

I closed the case, and tried to retape it, but the tape had lost its stick. ''Joe, have you got some more tape?''

''I think so. Let me take a look in the supply closet,'' he said as he left the room.

''You know, I think I saw the guy who owns that briefcase today—on my way over here, as a matter of fact,'' Tony said.

My heart skipped a beat. I stared at him in disbelief. ''Really?'' I asked, waiting for the other shoe to drop.

''Yeah. He was driving a gold Lincoln—beautiful car.

Only thing, the trunk was held closed with a bungee cord. The hood was wired closed with some bailing wire, and I think the only thing keeping the top on was luck.''

Once I realized he was teasing me, I relaxed and laughed along with him.

''You know, I could teach you how to pick those locks, so you don't have to destroy perfectly good briefcases,'' Tony said, his voice cracking with laughter.

''I just might take you up on that, Mr. Marino. The very next time I need to pick a lock, I'll give you a call.''

Tony pulled a business card from his wallet, and handed it to me. ''I certainly hope you will, Miss Lace. It would be my pleasure to assist you.''

Just then, Joe came back with a roll of tape. ''Here you go, Devonie—have a ball,'' he said as he handed it to me.

''Well, Joe. It appears my work here is done. I'd better get back to the office, before they all rob me blind,'' Tony said as he headed for the door. ''It was very nice to meet you, Devonie. Please don't hesitate to call me if you have any questions at all—and remember, if you decide you want to get rid of that thing, I'm sure I can get you a pretty penny for it.''

''Thanks, Tony. I'll let you know. It was nice meeting you, too.''

Joe walked his old friend out of the shop, then returned to the office, while I was securing the case.

''Oh, Devonie. I almost forgot. Here's your check for the ring,'' Joe said as he handed me an envelope with my name scrawled on it. Most people wouldn't cut a check for a consignee the very day of a sale, but Joe knows how tight finances are for me.

''Thanks, Joe. You've been a big help.''

Before I slipped the envelope and Tony's business card into my purse, I took a moment to read the card:

Anthony Marino
Importer and Exporter of Fine Goods

I wondered exactly what "fine goods" referred to, but decided not to pursue it just yet. I gave Joe a hug, and headed back to the Jeep. Something told me I had a big day ahead of me.

Tony Marino started the diesel engine of his Mercedes, and turned the volume down on the radio. He dialed a number on his cellular phone and waited for an answer. "Hello, Emilio? This is Marino. Is he in?"

"No, man. He had some business to take care of this morning."

"Tell your boss I think I've found that item he's been looking for. I'm pretty sure I can get my hands on it, but he's going to have to pay me top dollar for it. When he gets in, have him contact me for the details."

"Sure thing, Tony. I'll let him know."

Tony put the fine piece of German engineering into gear, and eased smoothly out onto the main street.

Chapter Six

I waved to Jason as I pulled into the parking lot in front of his shop. He was busy helping a customer load a refrigerator into the back of a pickup. He paused long enough to wave back to me. I quickly made my way to the warehouse. I sat down in front of the first safe, and removed the pages of the small address book from my purse. I tried the first combination of numbers. Nothing. I tried them a second time. Again—nothing. I closed my eyes, and said a little prayer before I tried the next combination. Very carefully, I turned the dial, being sure to stop exactly on the specified numbers. I grasped the handle and pulled. The door silently swung open. "Thank you," I said aloud as I peered inside the dark vault.

Anxiety kept my stomach feeling a little upset. I had visions of finding hand grenades, or sticks of dynamite inside the heavy metal box. I dreamed the night before that I opened it, and found a coiled, two-headed king cobra

inside. In my dream, it chased me all over the warehouse—
then it chased me all over San Diego. Finally, I ran until I
was waist-deep in the Pacific, hoping it couldn't swim. It
didn't come in after me. It just stayed on the beach, coiled,
and waiting for me to come out of the water.

Jason walked in, just in time to witness the opening of
the safe. "Way to go, Dev. What's in there?"

"I don't know yet. I just got it open," I answered. I
reached in, and pulled out a box about six inches by ten
inches. "What's this?" I asked.

He took it from me, and inspected it carefully. "I don't
know. It's some sort of electronic device, but I don't know
what it's for."

There was nothing else in the safe. "Well, let's see
what's in your box," I said as I got up, and moved over
to where the other safe sat. I worked the combination, and
it opened just as smoothly as the first one. Jason couldn't
hide the disappointment on his face. The box was empty—a
black hole.

"Gee, Jason. I'm sorry. But the safe is worth something.
Besides, now you have the combination," I consoled.

"Thanks, Dev. You're right. I can sell the safe in the
shop—or maybe I'll keep it for myself."

The bell rang from the shop, letting Jason know he had
a customer. "I'll be right back, Devonie. I want to talk to
you about what's going on with this stuff you picked up
yesterday," he said as he headed for the door.

I pulled a long, thin steel pin from my purse, and started
probing the lock on the file cabinet. I jiggled it, and wiggled
it back and forth. Finally, it clicked and the small metal
button popped out, just as if I had used a key.

I pulled the drawer open. The files were labeled by year.
They started with 1980, with the last file dated 1995.

I lifted out a thin folder from the 1980 section. It contained a single, brief newspaper clipping about a federal judge who had been shot to death in his home. The story went on to say that burglary seemed to be the motive, but there were no suspects in the case.

Each file contained similar accounts of important individuals who were killed, either by questionable means, or apparent accidents. Most were shootings in supposed robberies, or car accidents, a couple of suspected suicides, and one drowning.

As I read the accounts, my stomach began to feel a little queasy. I could sense small beads of sweat forming on my forehead and upper lip. I patted my face dry with a tissue, and read the last file. There was something different about this one. It wasn't about a single individual being killed. This article described an airline crash that happened a year ago—on a flight returning to Los Angeles from Mexico. The plane had somehow gotten off course, and flew into the side of a mountain. Everyone on board was killed. A thorough investigation performed by the FAA and the National Transportation Safety Board turned up nothing—at least nothing as far as a bomb or mechanical malfunction. Eventually, the authorities determined pilot error to be the cause of the crash, and the case was closed. Also in the file, I found a list of names: *Passenger list—Flight 9602*. There were two names highlighted in yellow. David Powers and Michael Norris. Who were they? By this time, I had figured out that Robert Kephart must be some sort of hired assassin, and this must be a recording of his achievements. Apparently he'd been in business since 1980, and performed anywhere from one to four of these ''services'' a year. David Powers and Michael Norris must have been his last assignment. Why would he kill all those people on the plane, if he were just after those two? This didn't make any sense. I put the files back into the cabinet, and locked it. I picked up the electronic box, and stowed it under my arm. Joe could probably help me identify it.

As I passed through the shop, I waved to Jason, who was busy helping a customer. "I've got to go, Jason. I'll call you later."

"Wait a minute, Dev. I want to talk to you." He turned and excused himself from his customer.

"I can't talk now, Jason. I've got to go, but I'll call you later. Okay?"

"Devonie, wait. I want you to tell me what's going on. Is everything all right?"

"I don't know, Jason. I'll call you when I know more," I called back as I hurried out of the shop.

I heard him curse between clenched teeth.

I laid the box on the seat next to me, and started the Jeep. I drove a short distance, to a small public park that's usually pretty quiet. I parked just in front of a pay phone situated near the corner of the block. I removed the pages of Robert Kephart's phone book from my purse, and made the call.

The phone rang many times before anyone answered. I had forgotten about the time difference between San Diego and Geneva, until the party at the other end of the line answered. A woman's raspy voice, barely audible, spoke into the receiver. I had obviously woken her up. "Hello," she repeated, trying to project a little more volume.

"Is this Kerstin Weibel?" I asked.

"Yes. This is Kerstin. Who am I speaking with?" the woman whispered.

"My name is Devonie. Do you know a Mr. Robert Kephart?"

There was a long silence. Finally, she spoke. "Who is this? How do you know Robert?" she demanded. Her voice echoed louder with each word spoken.

"I don't know him, but I think I've found something that belongs to him. Do you know how I can reach him?" I asked.

Again, she was silent. "Miss Weibel? Are you there?" I asked.

"Yes. I am here. What is it you've found?" she responded finally.

"It's of a particularly sensitive nature. I'd rather not say, until I can speak with Mr. Kephart. Is he there?" I asked.

"No. He is not here. I don't think you really want to have any contact with him. Won't you please tell me what this is about? You may be in danger."

"What kind of danger?" I asked.

"Well, tell me what it is you've found. For all I know, you may have just located his lost dry-cleaning claim ticket, and I have startled you for nothing."

"No. It's definitely not his laundry. Let's just say, I stumbled upon some equipment he had in storage. This stuff I found would hint that Mr. Kephart is no angel."

"I see," she replied. "I have a pretty good idea what it is you've found. You're right. Robert's no angel. He's extremely dangerous. If anyone in his circle finds out you have his belongings, you're in serious danger."

"Who are these people in his 'circle'?" I asked.

"Oh, they are all very bad people. Listen. What did you say your name was, again?"

"Devonie," I replied.

"Listen, Devonie. You can trust no one. People you think you can trust will turn out to be your worst nightmare. Believe me, I know. I've spent the last year on the run, hiding from these people. I've found only one person I can trust to keep me safe, and that's me. I can help you, too, if you'll let me.''

"How can you help me?" I asked.

"I can hide you, for a time. Most important, I can give you names, and show you pictures of the people you need to fear the most—the ones who will stop at nothing to get to you, and what you have."

A chill ran up my spine. I quickly scanned the area around the phone booth to see who might be watching me. I noticed an older man, walking his dog through the park, but he paid no attention to me.

"I have to think about this, Kerstin. As far as I know, no one knows what I have. If I find I need your help, can I reach you at this number?"

"Well, most any time—but during the waking hours would be preferable."

"I'm so sorry for waking you," I apologized.

A young man on a bicycle pedaled up to my Jeep, and stopped. I scrutinized his every move.

"I've got to go now, Kerstin. I'll be in touch." I hung up the phone and scurried back to the Jeep. The boy pedaled away as soon as he noticed me coming. I folded the pages from the address book, and slipped them into my jeans pocket.

I got in the Jeep, and drove back to Joe's shop. I wanted to see if he could help me identify the box I found in the safe. I was shocked to see police cars blocking the front of the shop, and yellow tape strung up all along the storefront. I parked as close as I could, and jogged across the street. Sarah was outside, sobbing as she talked to one of the policemen.

I caught the attention of one of the detectives, Jeffrey

McNight, according to his badge. "Excuse me. I'm a friend of Joe and Sarah. What's happened?"

"Your name?" he asked, as he took a small notepad and pencil from his pocket.

"Devonie Lace. I do business with Joe here in the shop. Is everything okay?"

"I'm sorry, ma'am. The proprietor of this establishment, Mr. Joe Barnes, was killed in what appears to be an attempted robbery," he explained.

My mouth fell open. I staggered back against the police car, bracing myself, so my knees wouldn't give out. Joe couldn't be dead. I must still be dreaming that crazy dream about the snakes. I felt a little dizzy, and the smell of exhaust from passing cars made me feel nauseated.

"Are you okay, miss?" he asked, as he took my arm and helped me to a bench.

"When did this happen? I was just here, talking to Joe this morning. Everything was fine when I left."

"We arrived twenty minutes ago. The call came in about five minutes before that. Can I ask what your business with Mr. Barnes was about?"

I didn't hear his question. A myriad of voices was harping at me in my head. I pictured a thousand scenarios of what might have happened to Joe, sure that I must somehow be responsible for his death. "I'm sorry. What did you say?" I asked.

"What was your business with Mr. Barnes this morning?" he repeated.

"Oh. He sold a ring for me. I came by to pick up the check."

"I see. Did you notice anyone, or anything unusual when you left?" he asked, as he scribbled on his notepad.

"No. I don't recall anything out of the ordinary." I tried

to remember if there were any customers in the shop when I left.

"And what time was it when you left here?"

"Let's see. I think it was about ten forty-five, maybe eleven o'clock. I'm not exactly sure."

Detective McNight noted what I told him. "Mrs. Lace, or is it Miss?" he asked.

"It's Miss," I replied.

"Miss Lace. Is there a number where we can reach you, in case we have any more questions?"

"Yes. Of course," I answered, and gave him my number.

Then he handed me a card with his name and number on it. "If you think of anything that might be of relevance, please call me."

"I will," I assured him, as I took the card and placed it in my purse.

I walked over to Sarah, and put my arm around her shoulders. "Oh, Sarah. I'm so sorry. I just can't believe this has happened."

"Oh, Devonie," she sobbed.

"Listen, Sarah. If you need anything, just let me know. I have lots of free time, and I can help you make arrangements, or contact relatives—whatever you need. Okay?"

"Thank you. I appreciate that, Devonie," she said, then blew her nose into an already overextended tissue. I reached into my purse, and took out a small pack of Kleenex.

"Here, Sarah." I handed them to her. "Whoever did this, did they take anything from the store?"

"No. Margo was in the back, writing up the bank deposit slip, when she heard a shot. She run out to see what it was, and found my Joe lying on the floor, behind the counter.

Whoever did it must have gotten scared and run, because Margo said the place was empty.''

''I just can't believe this is happening. Sarah, do you have someone to stay with you? You don't want to be alone right now.''

''Yes. My sister is driving down from Los Angeles this afternoon, and my son is flying in tonight from San Antonio.'' She started crying again. ''Oh, Devonie. I just don't know what I'm going to do without my Joe.''

''I know, Sarah—he was a good man. But you'll be fine. We'll all see to that. Anything you need, I want you to let me know. Okay?''

''Okay, sweetheart. Devonie, you're a good girl,'' she said as she sobbed into a fresh tissue.

Detective McNight marched over, and put a hand on Sarah's shoulder. ''Mrs. Barnes. We just have a few more questions for you, then I'll have one of the officers take you home. Will you please excuse us, Miss Lace?''

''Certainly,'' I replied, as I gave Sarah a hug. My heart ached as I watched her leave with the detective.

It finally struck me that my dear friend was gone—forever. Tears began to well up and run down my cheeks as I crossed the street. A car horn blared at me as I hurried to get out of its way. Visions of the two-headed snake flashed back into my head.

Chapter Seven

Guadalajara—1995

Frank Eastwood, the first FAA inspector to arrive at the crash site, walked stiffly around the rubble. The location was so remote, he had to be brought in on horseback—a form of transportation he wasn't accustomed to. The twenty-year veteran had earned the respect of every official in the organization.

By the time the others arrived, he had already sifted through much of the wreckage. He had located the black box, and was arranging to have it transported as soon as possible, so it could be evaluated.

Dozens of people were working to locate and remove the charred bodies of the passengers and crew. This was always the first priority. Frank never got involved in the removal of the dead. As many crashes as he had seen throughout the years, he could never get used to seeing the victims.

His sole responsibility would be to determine the cause of the crash. Was it pilot error? Mechanical failure? Was it an act of terrorism? These were the questions Frank struggled to answer.

So far, he had found nothing to lead him to any conclusions. He wandered downhill, away from the crash site, and started kicking the dirt around in a clump of charred trees. Something shiny caught his eye—the mangled remains of a metal box that appeared to have had a run-in with a tree— and the tree had won. Frank inspected it suspiciously, bagged it up, and noted a description of the strange item for his preliminary report. It would have to be sent back, along with the black box, and inspected closer to be identified. Frank knew it wasn't any standard equipment from the airliner. He was intimately familiar with every piece of airplane hardware—from the computerized navigation devices, down to the toilet-flush handles. After careful consideration, Frank decided to deliver this item to the lab himself, rather than sending it down with the black box. He put it in his pack, and continued his investigation.

When Frank arrived at his office in D.C., his superior, along with high-ups from both the FBI and CIA, were waiting for him. "Hello, Frank. What's the word on the Mexico disaster?" Carl Hobson, director of the CIA, asked—even before Frank had a chance to sit down.

"I'm just fine, Carl. How are you and the wife and kids?" Frank replied, doing little to ease the tension in the room. Frank was not the type to be pressured or rushed. When he was ready to give his opinion, he would put it all in his report, and make it part of the official record. Until then, he wasn't about to speculate, or jump to conclusions.

"Sorry, Frank. We're just anxious to get to the bottom

of this incident. The crew on that flight was one of the most experienced in the field. The White House wants to assure the American public it wasn't a bomb, or some other form of terrorism. We can't have the whole country getting nervous, and afraid to fly because of this.''

Frank opened his pack, and placed the mangled metal box on his desk. ''I'm not so sure the American public shouldn't be nervous about flying—especially when something like this can be placed in the baggage compartment, without being noticed.''

They stared in silence. ''Is it a bomb?'' one of them asked.

Frank shook his head. ''No. It's not a bomb. To be honest, I don't know for sure what it is. I don't want to say what I think it might be, at least until the guys in the lab have a look. For all I know, it might be part of some new sort of stereo equipment.''

Frank's boss, Hal, picked up the box, and carefully inspected it. ''Frank, I'm going to have Clara take this down to the lab right now, while we're meeting. The sooner they get on this, the better. I'll be right back,'' he said as he left the room with the box. The discussion continued during his absence. By the time Hal returned, Frank was ready to dismiss everyone, so he could get to work.

''If you gentlemen will excuse me, I have a lot of work to do, so I can have a preliminary report ready for you. I was planning to leave for a vacation next week, but I guess I'll put that on hold till we get this ironed out,'' Frank informed the group.

Hal spoke up. ''I don't think that'll be necessary, Frank. You can take a couple of days to put together your preliminary report, and the boys in the lab can put the rest of the picture together. Go ahead and take your vacation. When you get back, everything should be ready for your final stamp of approval, and we can put this thing to bed.''

Frank curiously eyed his boss. It wasn't like Hal to be generous with time off. If he had his way, no one would ever take a vacation, a sick day, or for that matter, a weekend off. ''That's okay, Hal. I can reschedule for another time. It isn't as though I have reservations, or airline tickets purchased, or anything like that.''

''No. I insist. If I ruin this vacation for Helen, I'll never hear the end of it. Your wife will tell my wife what an ogre I am, and I'll be sleeping on the couch for the next three months.''

''Well, okay, Hal. If you insist,'' Frank replied, still a little confused, but pleased just the same. It was true, the personnel in the lab had the most work to do on this case.

''Where are you going this year?'' Carl asked.

''Helen and I are taking a trip up to Alaska. I've been wanting to take the Thorp on an extended flight.''

''Really? That's a pretty small plane, isn't it? How are you going to carry the required survival gear over Canadian airspace, and still have room for luggage?''

Frank chuckled to himself before he replied. ''I had a heck of a time convincing Helen we should take the Thorp. She wanted to cruise the inside passage, and go in luxury. I had to promise her when we get there, I'll buy her a whole new wardrobe. Before we return home, we'll have to have all her new clothes shipped back here.''

''Big mistake, Frank. You should've done the inside passage—would've saved yourself a bunch of money,'' his boss joked. The group laughed as they filed out of Frank's office.

* * *

Frank laid the preliminary report on his boss's desk. "Here you go, Hal. When I get back from Alaska, I'll go over the data with the boys from the lab, and we'll put our stamp of approval on it."

"Thanks, Frank. You and Helen have a good time, and be careful."

"I will. See you in a couple of weeks."

Frank picked Helen up, and drove straight to the airport. He had already loaded the plane with survival gear and fuel. He just wanted to do a last-minute check of the engine, to make sure everything was in good condition. Helen sat in the cockpit, reading one of her romance novels while she waited. Frank had built this little experimental plane from the ground up—he was intimately familiar with every single detail on it. Frank's keen eyes carefully felt their way over every hose and line, every nut and bolt, every rivet and fastener. He noticed something unusual, and pulled a screwdriver from his tool kit. He removed a small object from an obscure section of the oil line. He inspected it carefully, then walked over to the opened Plexiglas cockpit.

"Helen, get out of the plane," he ordered.

"What's the matter?" she asked, as she climbed out onto the wing, and stepped gingerly down onto the asphalt.

"I forgot something at the office. Why don't you have a cup of coffee, over in the coffee shop, while I run back and get it."

"Okay, honey. What did you forget that's so important?" she asked. Helen tried to remember the last time Frank forgot something. She struggled to recall *any* time Frank forgot something. It had never happened, as far as she could remember.

"I'll tell you later. Could you keep an eye on the plane

from the coffee shop for me? Just make sure no one comes around it. I'd hate to lose any of our gear.''

''Sure, honey,'' she said as she marked her place in the novel, and headed for the airport restaurant—still puzzled by her husband's abrupt change of plans.

Frank returned to the office, and walked silently down to the lab, avoiding being seen by anyone. He peered through the window in the door. Hal sat on a workbench, his back to the door. He fingered the electronic box from the crash site with one hand, and held the phone to his ear with the other. Frank watched him for several moments. When he hung up the phone, he stood, placed the box under his arm, and explained to the lab personnel why he was taking it. Frank ducked away from the door, and out of the hallway before Hal exited the lab.

Frank made his way quietly back to his office, and pulled a file from his cabinet. He carried the preliminary report on the Guadalajara accident to a copy machine, and began making copies. When he heard footsteps coming toward the copy room, he quickly ducked around the corner, behind a large file cabinet.

Hal's secretary approached the busy copy machine, and watched curiously as it proceeded to make dozens of copies, while unattended. She looked around the room to see who was minding this job. She looked at the stack of documents she had to copy, then checked her watch, and decided to use the copy machine at the other end of the office.

Frank breathed a sigh of relief, and emerged from behind the file cabinet. He hoped she hadn't paid enough attention to the machine to notice the specifics of the documents being copied. When the machine finished, he gathered up everything, and slipped back to his office. He replaced the original report in his file cabinet, and placed the copies in his flight case. Frank left the building, having gone unnoticed, and returned to the airport.

"Helen. Did anyone go near the plane?"

"No. I watched it the whole time. What's wrong, Frank? You're acting very strange."

"I'll explain after we get in the air. I just want to go over the Thorp one more time before we take off."

Four hours later, after he had practically taken the whole plane apart and put it back together, he was satisfied that all was safe.

"Okay. Hop in. Let's go," he said to Helen, who had finished her novel, and was starting a new one.

"No way, mister. You're crazy if you think I'm getting in that plane, the way you're acting. You've just given it the bomb-sniffing-dog treatment, and I'm not stepping one foot closer to it until you tell me what's going on."

Frank explained that he had discovered a barometric pressure–sensitive explosive device attached to the oil line during his first inspection. It was a small explosive—just enough to rupture the oil line, and cause engine failure. It probably wouldn't have been triggered until the plane was going over the highest mountains of their trip, where an emergency landing would be impossible.

Helen struggled to form words from the myriad of thoughts racing through her head. "Why in the . . . Whatever would . . . Who in the world would do something like that, Frank?"

"I don't know for sure, but I have a suspicion. Anyhow, the plane is perfectly safe now. You have to trust me. The safest thing we can do is just get out of here. I have a plan. I'll explain it on the way. I need you to be with me on this, Helen. Right?"

"Right," she echoed. Helen's sense of adventure overpowered her desire to be cautious. She remembered why she ran off and eloped with this daredevil air force pilot, so long ago. "Oh, why not. It's sure to be exciting. Beats the heck out of these crazy dime-store romance novels."

The Thorp taxied to the runway and took off, headed northwest. The one-hundred-eighty-mile-per-hour cruising speed allowed Frank several days to formulate his plan. Frank and Helen came up with a scheme they thought would be effective. They practiced it several times, then, when the time was right, set it into motion.

Somewhere over Canadian airspace, Frank got on the radio to flight service. "Mayday! Mayday! This is Thorp N4075K. I have an emergency! I've lost all oil pressure, and my engine has stalled. I'm on a flight plan from Port Hardy to Prince Rupert. There's nothing in sight but mountains, trees, lakes, and a whole lot of ocean. I'm going down! I'm going down!" Frank shouted. He even had Helen a little nervous.

Helen played along, and screamed as if she were a hysterical passenger—faced with impending disaster. "Oh, no! We're going to die! We're going to die! Frank, you jerk! I told you I wanted to take a cruise. You should've listened to me. Now, look. This is all your fault. We're going to die, and I haven't even seen Graceland yet!" Helen frantically exclaimed. She picked up a map, and bonked Frank on the head with it.

Frank ducked her swat, eyeing her with surprise.

"Oops. Sorry," she mouthed, realizing she had gotten a little carried away with her role.

Frank announced again that his engine had quit, and he was going down. Finally, he cut the radio off, and changed his course. The next time the little plane would get an extended rest would be in the Bahamas.

Chapter Eight

I parked the Jeep in the marina parking lot. I pulled the briefcase, and the U.E.B.—that's short for unidentified electronic box, an acronym Jason came up with to help put a name to it—from the passenger seat. The tape wasn't holding very well, so I carried the case hugged close to my body, like a bag of groceries. It was nearly dusk and the sunset on the Pacific was particularly breathtaking. I made my way down past the marina office when I noticed two men stepping onto my boat. I quickly sidestepped behind the office, and peered around the corner to see what they were up to. They were too far away to see any real details, and I couldn't hear them at all. One was tall and slender, and wore a ponytail. The other was shorter and stocky, with a shiny, shaved head. My heart pounded. What were they doing? I could see the tall one trying to get down below.

The other man appeared to be searching around the deck for something.

For a brief moment, I contemplated taking the gun from its case, marching bravely down the dock, and confronting the pair. Luckily, Mr. Cartwright appeared on the scene and interrupted the intruders before I mustered up the courage to play policewoman. I couldn't hear the conversation, but I could see my neighbor pointing in the direction of the Grille restaurant, and then toward the marina office. I quickly ducked back behind the wall before they spotted me. I counted to twenty, then slowly peered back around the corner to see what was going on. The two men were climbing off my boat. Mr. Cartwright watched as they made their way back up the dock toward the marina office. I slipped behind a tall bush growing in a planter next to the front door. As the pair passed, I could hear bits of their conversation.

"We'll have to come back later, when the nosy old guy is sleeping," the taller one said.

"I don't see why we couldn't have just taken him out. That's what we're supposed to do to the girl after we find the money, anyway. Right?"

"You idiot. It's almost broad daylight. You think shooting the old guy right there would have gone unnoticed? I swear. You're so stupid, you couldn't pour beer out of a boot if the directions were written on the heel."

"I could so. And one more thing. If he shows up tonight, when we come back, I'm shooting the old guy right between the eyes."

"Just shut up!"

Those were the last words I could hear clearly. I stayed behind the bush, and watched as the pair got into a black

BMW with tinted windows. They sped off, out of my view in less than a minute.

I hurried down the dock, and stopped in front of Mr. Cartwright's boat. "Good evening, Miss Lace. A couple of friends of yours were just here looking for you. They seemed a little insistent on staying on your boat, but I convinced them to come back later—when you were here. They just left. In fact, I'm surprised you didn't pass them on your way in."

"Really? Did they say what they wanted, or who they were?" I asked.

"No. Just that they were friends of yours from way back, and they wanted to invite you to some sort of party or reunion or something. Funny, they didn't exactly look like the type of fellows you would hang out with. Kind of rough-looking. You know."

"Hmm. Doesn't sound like anyone I know. Maybe some customers from the Grille found out I live here. I've heard from other waitresses that some of the customers like to harass them. Thanks for setting them straight about hanging out on my boat. I don't really care to have strangers loitering around here."

"Anytime, Miss Lace. I'm not exactly wild about having those types hanging around here, either. Maybe you should look for some other form of employment, if the clientele are going to become a problem."

I didn't answer him. I just smiled, and nodded as I stepped onto my boat with my case and mystery box in tow.

Everything seemed to be where I left it when I departed this morning. The other case and the computer were still sitting safely in my closet. I stowed the second case and the U.E.B. in the closet next to them, and shut the door. It would be dark soon—I had to act quickly.

I checked my fuel level. The tank was nearly empty. I didn't have time to stop and fuel up; I had to get out of the marina, before it was too dark to see. I started the engine and checked my gauges. Quickly, I scooted along the rail toward the bow, and untied the line to the dock. I pulled up the fenders as I made my way back to the stern, and liberated my boat from the confines of the dock. I slowly backed out of my slip, as Mr. Cartwright looked on with undivided attention. I waved and smiled as I carefully made my way around all the obstacles in the marina, and headed out toward the open sea.

I could still see the lights of the marina by the time the sun was completely down, but I felt I was out far enough to be safe tonight. I didn't dare go any farther, with my fuel situation the way it was. I dropped anchor, and settled in for the night. I didn't have a plan yet, but I was working on one.

I called Jason's number, and he picked up on the third ring. "Hey, Jason. It's me, Devonie."

"Dev. What's going on?"

"I'm out on my boat right now. Listen, Jason. I need you to do me a favor."

"Sure, Dev. What is it?"

"Can you get over to the marina and get my Jeep? I need you to take it over to your place tonight. You know where I keep the spare key, don't you?" I asked.

"Yeah. I remember where you keep it. What's going on, Dev? Why can't you bring it over yourself?"

"I'm literally out on my boat, Jason. You have to bring the Jeep to me, when I decide where I'm going. Right now, I need to get it away from the marina. Listen, Jason. I need you to do it now, while it's early, not later tonight. Is that okay?''

Jason paused, gathered up his nerve, then answered in the sternest voice he could muster. ''No, Dev. I'm not doing another thing for you until you tell me what's going on.''

''Jason. I promise I'll tell you everything when I see you tomorrow. But right now, I need your help. Will you do it for me? Please?''

He buckled, as usual. ''Okay, Dev. But this is the last time, unless you keep your promise and tell me what the devil is going on. Understand?''

''I understand. Listen, Jason. You need to get over there right away. If you see anyone hanging around my slip, just leave. Don't go anywhere near them, and don't let them see you take my Jeep. I'll call you tomorrow when I dock to let you know where to bring it.''

''Okay, Dev. You'd better keep your promise.''

''I will. Thanks, Jason. Please be careful. Remember what I said about any strangers hanging around—they could be dangerous. 'Bye, Jason,'' I said, and powered off my cell phone.

I made a sandwich, and took a bottle of water from the refrigerator. I rifled through a stack of books I kept in a cupboard over the dining table. ''Ah, there it is,'' I said as I pulled the book down from the shelf. ''*The Fine Art of Sailing.*'' I had picked it up just before I bought the *Plan B,* but hadn't had a chance to read it. I settled down in a chair on the deck with a lantern, my dinner, and the book, and started to read.

It was past eleven when I finally checked my watch. I closed the book, picked up my empty plate and the lantern, and went inside. I lay in bed, noticing every movement of the boat. It was very dark and quiet out here. I dozed off a couple of times, but a disturbing dream kept jarring me out of my sleep. Around 3:00 A.M., as I tried to fall back to sleep, I heard the faint sound of an engine in the distance. I got up, and felt my way to the door. I didn't want to put on my anchor lights, but I didn't want any boats to run into me, either. I scanned the horizon in the direction of the sound, and spotted lights coming toward me. Would those two thugs actually procure a boat, and come looking for me? That was ridiculous. They could have no hope of finding me out in the vast ocean, in the middle of the night. I was just being paranoid. But still, I watched as the vessel made its way past my position, and proceeded to the north—probably headed for Catalina Island. I went back to bed, and tried to think of a plan.

It seemed like an eternity before the sun finally began to peek over the horizon to the east. I sat up in my bunk, and peered out the window to check the weather. It was barely light enough to make out the shape of something strange, just off of the starboard side. I strained my eyes to focus on the object. *Uh-oh. It's a boat.* I jumped out of bed, frantically searching for my deck shoes. Just as I got the second one on, I could see the hatch door latch turn. I couldn't breathe. I couldn't move. I just sat there, paralyzed with fear. Then I heard a familiar voice inside my head telling me, *Don't panic. Never panic. It won't help.*

The ugly, scarred face of the ponytailed thug smirked at me through the open hatch. "Top of the morning to you, ma'am. Permission to board?"

"It's a little late to ask permission. Looks like you're already on board, to me," I said with a sneer.

"That it does. Well, how about permission to come below?"

"Get off my boat," I growled.

"Is that any way to talk to a guest?" he shot back, with all the charm of a rattlesnake.

He started down the steps. I thought of the gun sitting in my closet. The case was wrapped in duct tape. I could never get it open, let alone remove and load the gun before he got to me. He stepped off the last stair, and gazed around at the interior of the *Plan B*.

"My. What a neat boat you have here. Must be nice to be able to just up and set sail, whenever you want."

"What do you want?" I demanded.

"Want? What makes you think I want something? My friend and I were just out messing around, and saw this cool boat. We thought you might be in trouble, or need some help. Out here all alone?"

"I don't need any help. Now get off my boat."

"Okay. Just settle down. I'll leave in a minute, but first, how about a little breakfast? My friend and me, we're real hungry. We've been out all night looking for . . . for whales, yeah, that's it, we're whale watching."

"You're not going to see any whales around here this time of year. Where's this friend you keep talking about?" I asked. Then I saw the feet and legs of his partner through the window. He was up on the deck, making his way to the bow of the boat.

"Really? No whales? Where do I have to go to see whales?"

I scowled at him. My cell phone was sitting in its charger on the galley table. I couldn't get to it without going past him. Even if I could, I didn't know who I would call. No one could get here in time to help me. He started walking toward me. As he approached, I made a dive for the galley table, and scrambled under it. He grabbed my ankle, and tried to pull me back. I struggled and kicked hard enough to hit him in the face with my free foot. He let go of my leg, and held his hands to his bleeding nose.

"Aargh! I think you broke my nose." He cursed as he struggled to his feet.

I sprang out from under the table and lunged to the hatch door. He caught the fabric of my T-shirt with one hand and pulled me back against him. He removed a gun he had tucked into the back of his pants and began waving it in my face.

"You're gonna pay for this, lady," he threatened. "You broke my nose."

I didn't have time to think of any elaborate plan. If I was going to get out of this, I would have to act quickly. I saw it sitting there on the counter where I had left it the night before. In one swift motion, I grabbed the fishbowl, and swung it hard against his head. He fell to the floor, along with a thousand pieces of broken glass.

"There. Now we're even," I announced. "I broke your nose, and you broke my fishbowl."

His partner heard the commotion. "Hey, Tommy. What's going on down there? You take care of her yet?" he called from up on the deck.

I snatched the gun from the unconscious thug's hand, and hurried up the steps to the deck.

Baldy was hanging over the side, losing his dinner—not paying any attention to me. With trembling hands, I aimed the weapon at him.

"Get your hands in the air, and face me," I demanded.

Slowly, he straightened up and stared at me. "Whoa. C'mon, lady. Don't shoot."

"Just keep your hands over your head, and slowly walk to me," I ordered.

The boat rocked. He started to put his hands down, to grab the rail. I fired the gun over his head. "I told you, keep your hands in the air. I'm serious."

"Okay. Okay. Just please, don't shoot me." He whimpered.

"Get yourself over here now, and I won't shoot you."

He scooted his way back to me. I took the gun he had holstered under his arm. I was wearing only the long T-shirt I had slept in, and my deck shoes. There was no place to safely tuck the weapon on my body. I was afraid to leave it on deck, in case one of them managed to get their hands on it. Reluctantly, I threw it overboard. I motioned for him to go down below, through the hatch door.

"Get your friend, and bring him up here," I ordered.

Thug number two looked down into the galley, and saw his partner lying in a pile of broken glass, with blood running from his nose. "You've killed him. Are you crazy, lady? You've killed Tommy. The boss is really going to freak now."

"Settle down. He's not dead. Just get down there, and drag him up. Now!" I shouted.

He carried Tommy up the steps, and laid him on one of the cushioned seats. I kept the gun pointed at him as I stepped off the *Plan B,* onto the *Sea Ray* they had obviously stolen from the marina. I tossed a life jacket into the water. I pulled the keys from the ignition, and threw them overboard as well. Then I climbed back onto my boat and untied the *Sea Ray,* shoving it away as hard as I could.

"Bring him over here," I said as I waved the gun at the whimpering, seasick, lowlife scum who was polluting my boat. *What a waste of skin,* I thought to myself.

He hoisted his partner onto his shoulder, and carried him over to the rail.

"Now toss him over."

"What?"

"You heard me. I said toss him over; then, you next."

"He'll drown."

"No, he won't. There's a life jacket out there. You can take care of him. Now get him off my boat."

Again, I waved the gun at him. He dropped his partner into the water, then jumped in after him. I watched as he struggled to reach the life jacket. I pulled up my anchor, and started the engine. I had only a few minutes of fuel left, so I cut it off when I was far enough away from them to be safe. I quickly cleaned up the fishbowl glass, while I formulated my short-term plan.

I raised my sails, opened up my *How to Sail* book, and headed north. My aunt and uncle have a house on the ocean near Del Mar. They have their own private little harbor and dock. They'd repeatedly invited me to sail up for a visit. I'd only been there by car, so I didn't know how I would find it from here. I figured when I got in the general vicinity, I would call and ask directions.

An hour ticked by when my stomach started growling, then I realized I hadn't eaten breakfast. I secured the wheel and went down to the galley for some fruit. I was feeling quite smug that I had taken care of those two morons— and on top of that, I was sailing my boat successfully. I flipped on the stereo, so I could hear it on deck. I climbed back out onto the deck with my apple and glass of juice. I checked over my shoulder. Yes, the land was still over there, so I was going in the right direction. I turned, and stepped just in time for the boom to swing around, and hit me square in the forehead. Bad karma is the price I pay for smugness.

When I came to, I had a pretty good-sized lump on my

head—and one whopper of a headache. Broken glass and orange juice littered the deck. When I stood up, the boat began spinning, as if caught in a whirlpool. I reached to grab the rail to catch myself, but I fell back down on the deck. The palm of my hand landed squarely on a piece of sharp glass and made a rather deep gash that gushed blood. Finally, the boat quit spinning. I crawled back down to the galley, and pulled myself up to the sink. I ran water over my throbbing hand, and looked around for a clean towel to wrap it in. I had a first-aid kit in the head, but I was still too dizzy to maneuver my way around the boat. I got back down on the floor, and crawled to the head. I managed to get the first-aid kit open with my one good hand, and cleaned and dressed my wound the best I could. I looked out the window. I was still sailing full blast ahead, with no land in sight. I made my way back up to the deck. I brought the sails down, and dropped anchor so I could clean up the mess, and try to get my bearings. I checked my watch. I had been sailing aimlessly for several hours. I had no idea where I was. I checked my compass. I was currently headed southwest. The Santa Ana winds were blowing, which are predominantly from the northeast. For all I knew, I could have been sailing in circles for the last four hours. I checked my fuel level. I estimated about ten minutes of fuel left. I got myself turned around, set my sails, and headed northeast. Eventually, I would come to land. The only question, would it be Long Beach, or Baja?

When I finally got close enough, I looked through my binoculars toward the land and scanned the coast. I spotted a restaurant, with its own dock, a little to the north. I could barely make out the name on the sign. It looked like "Swordfish Café."

I dropped sails again, to make a call. "Hello. Aunt Arlene?"

"Yes. Is this Devonie or Monica?" she asked.

"It's Devonie, Aunt Arlene. Are you and Uncle Doug going to be home for a little while?"

"Yes. We don't have any plans to go out. Are you coming over?"

"Well, I hope so. I'm on my boat right now, hopefully headed in your direction. Remember that restaurant you and Uncle Doug took me to last year? We were celebrating my purchase of the *Plan B*. I think it was called the Swordfish Café?"

"Oh, yes. Wasn't that the best dinner you ever had? I just love that restaurant. We go there at least once a month."

"Well, I'm directly west of that place. I need to know how to get to your house from here."

"Oh, honey. Let me get Doug to direct you. Hang on just a minute," she said, and then called to her husband.

Uncle Doug wanted to fax me a map. I had to explain I didn't have a fax machine on the boat. He communicated the directions to me, and then I wrote them on a piece of scratch paper I found in the galley.

"Thanks, Uncle Doug. I'll see you in a little while," I said, then powered off the phone.

My head ached, and at times I saw two of everything—making it hard to head toward landmarks. I finally cruised into the small private harbor that belonged to my aunt and uncle. I dropped the sails, and powered up the engine so I could maneuver to the dock. Doug and Arlene were waiting for me on the small pier. I threw them my lines. They tied up my boat while I set the fenders.

Uncle Doug owns a yacht brokerage in Del Mar. It's

quite a lucrative business for him. He helped me find the *Plan B,* in a small marina up in San Francisco. He told me that if I didn't buy her, he was going to snatch her up himself. She was such a sweet deal.

"Devonie. Get down off that beautiful boat. I've made lunch reservations for us at the Turf Club. We're going to the horse races," Uncle Doug announced, as I shut down the engine and stepped off the boat.

"How fun," I said, "but I don't feel too good right now."

"What's wrong? Hey—what's that big bump on your head?" Uncle Doug asked.

"Just call me Devonie '*Boom-Boom*' Lace, master sailor."

"No. You didn't get hit with the boom. Did you?"

"Yes. I did. And I think I might have a concussion. I'm seeing double, and I feel like I have to throw . . . well, you know the feeling. On top of that, I fell and cut my hand on some broken glass. I think I might need some stitches," I said, holding my throbbing, bandaged hand in front of his concerned eyes.

Aunt Arlene took me by the arm. "Oh, honey. We'd better get you inside to lie down. Our next-door neighbor is a doctor. Doug, why don't you call Craig, and see if he'll come over to look at this?"

Uncle Doug grinned at Arlene. "Oh sure, Arlene. Or we could take her to the emergency room, but there might not be any nice, single young doctors like Craig, there."

"Now, you just hush. Craig is a fine doctor, and he can probably be here in five minutes. I'm only thinking of Devonie."

"I'm sure you are. I'll call Craig right now."

Aunt Arlene led me into a living room so exquisite, you

would swear you'd seen it in *Better Homes and Gardens.* Come to think of it, I believe it was featured in the Christmas issue, two years ago. One wall, windows from floor to ceiling, overlooked the ocean. The oak floors, finished in a light, natural tone, gave the room a warm, homey feeling. A sea-foam green and blue rug relaxed under the fine sofa and coffee table facing the view. You could sit for hours and admire the living landscape, painted just outside the glass. The open beam ceiling, also finished in natural tones, gave the feeling of a cathedral. Everything in the room said, "This house belongs to a sailor," from the paintings on the walls, to the trophies on the mantel. Arlene sat me down on the sofa. "Now, you just sit here. I don't think you're supposed to lie down or go to sleep—at least until we have the doctor look at you first."

"Okay, Aunt Arlene. I'm just going to close my eyes for a minute. I didn't sleep very well last night, and I'm so tired."

The next thing I remembered was a hand shaking my shoulder, and a voice calling my name. I opened my eyes. There were three concerned faces staring at me. Uncle Doug, Aunt Arlene, and in the middle, a handsome face I didn't recognize. "Mel? Is that you?" I mumbled, only half-conscious.

Chapter Nine

Mild concussion was the diagnosis. Rest was the treatment. Craig Matthews, the doctor who lived next door, stitched up my hand and gave it a proper dressing. I used Uncle Doug's phone to call Jason, since I had left my cell phone on the boat, and didn't feel quite up to hiking back down to the dock to retrieve it.

"Hello, Jason. It's Devonie."

"Dev. Where are you?" he asked.

"I'm at my aunt and uncle's place in Del Mar. Did you have any trouble getting the Jeep?"

"No. I rode my bike over to the marina, loaded it in the back, and brought it home. No one gave me any trouble."

"That's good. Listen, Jason, I was going to see if you could bring it here today, but I had a little accident, and I wouldn't be able to drive you back home until tomorrow or the next day."

"Accident? What sort of accident? Are you okay?" he questioned.

"Oh, I'm okay. I got hit in the head with the boom, and I have a mild concussion. I'll be fine by tomorrow or the next day, but for now I'm seeing double, and I'm a little dizzy, so I can't get behind the wheel," I explained.

"Do you want me to bring it up to you Wednesday morning? I could get John to open the shop for me. That would give you a full day to recover."

"Yeah. I think that would work. Let me get my uncle to give you directions on how to get here," I said, and handed the phone to Doug. I leaned back on the couch with an ice pack on my forehead, and closed my eyes.

Doug gave detailed directions to Jason, while Arlene thanked Craig for making the house call. "Would you like to stay for dinner, Craig?" I heard her ask him. I knew what she was up to.

"I wish I could, Arlene, but I have to attend a retirement dinner tonight for one of the doctors at the med center. I'll check in on our patient tonight when I get back, and again in the morning, to make sure she's progressing okay."

"Thank you, Craig," I called to him, not taking the ice pack from my head.

"Anytime, Devonie. You take it easy. I'll check in on you tonight," he called back to me, then closed the door behind him.

Jason arrived Wednesday morning with the Jeep. I introduced him to Arlene and Doug. They gave him a brief tour of the house. I said I would show him the dock, so I could have a chance to talk to him alone.

"Thanks again for getting the Jeep, Jason. I can't tell

you how much I appreciate all your help,'' I told him, as we walked down the path to the dock.

''You're welcome, Dev. Now, are you going to tell me what's going on?''

''Okay, but you have to promise to keep this to yourself.''

''You know I will.''

''Remember those cases I got at the auction? One of them had a half a million dollars in it. The other one had a nine-millimeter gun with a laser sighting scope, and a silencer.''

''Come on, Dev. Quit kidding around. You promised you'd tell me what was going on,'' he complained.

''I'm not kidding, Jason. What's more, I showed the gun to Joe, over at the pawnshop. He had one of his old-time war buddies look at it, and now Joe is dead. When I went back to my boat, there were two characters snooping around, trying to get in. I overheard them saying that they were supposed to 'take me out,' after they got the money. That's why I took off in the boat—to come here. They followed me and boarded my boat while I was sleeping. I managed to get them off, but I'm really scared, Jason.'' My voice trembled.

''What? You're serious. Joe is *dead*? For Pete's sake, Devonie. Why haven't you gone to the police?''

''I don't know. I guess at first I was afraid they would make me give up the money. But now, after what happened to Joe, I think I'd better go to the FBI or CIA, or whoever the heck you go to when you're afraid for your life.''

''Why the FBI or CIA? Why not just go to the police?''

''That file cabinet that I stored in your warehouse is full of newspaper clippings. They all describe the deaths of quite a few prominent people, over the last fifteen years.

Remember that plane crash in Mexico last year, the one that killed all those people on board?''

"Yeah. The one where the pilots got off-course somehow, and plowed into the side of a mountain?''

"That's the one. That was the last article. Whoever rented that storage unit was a hired assassin, and the plane crash was his last job.''

"This is incredible. But who killed Joe, and why?''

"I don't know why, but the only other person who knew about the gun was Joe's friend, Tony Marino.''

"Tony Marino?''

"Yeah. Have you heard of him?''

"That friend of mine I told you about, the one who works for the San Diego Police Department, he told me about a local mobster named Tony Marino. He has some sort of export business that he uses for a front, but his ties to the mob go pretty deep. If he knows about you and the gun and the money, then I'd say you're in quite a bit of danger.''

"I didn't tell him or Joe about the money. I don't see why anyone would kill Joe just because he knew I had the gun.''

We got to the end of the dock, and stepped onto the deck of my boat. Jason opened the hatch, and we went below to the galley.

"Sit down there. I want to get that electronic box and the computer before we head back to San Diego," I said as I made my way back to my cabin. I opened the closet doors. Everything seemed to be in order. I grabbed the two items and closed the doors again.

"I want to see if I can get a power cord for this laptop. The battery is dead, and I can't power it up. I guess I'll

take this mystery box to the FBI. Maybe they can identify it.''

"That's a good idea. What about the money? Do you
still have it with you?''

"Are you kidding? I put it in a safe-deposit box. It's
going to stay there until this thing blows over—if I can
help it.''

We walked back up the dock to the house. I handed
Jason the computer and the electronic box. "Here. You
take this stuff to the Jeep. I just want to let Arlene and
Doug know I'm taking you back home. I'll be right there.''

"You mean your friend isn't staying for lunch?'' Arlene
asked when we were inside. Her disappointment showed.

"No, Aunt Arlene. I need to get him home, and I have
some business to take care of in San Diego. I shouldn't be
too late, but don't hold dinner for me, in case I get tied
up.''

"Okay, honey. How's your head? Are you sure you
should be driving? Maybe we should just have Craig come
over, and take a quick look before you go.''

"I feel fine today. I'm sure I'm completely recovered.
Besides, I saw Craig leave a little while ago. He must have
gone to work. I'll see you later, Aunt Arlene. 'Bye.''

" 'Bye.''

We stopped at Jason's warehouse first, and picked up the
newspaper clippings from the file cabinet. Jason insisted on
going with me to the FBI office.

I briefly explained to the man at the front desk about the
gun, and the newspaper clippings, and Joe's death, and the
two strangers on my boat. He directed us to have a seat,
then he called someone on the phone. Several minutes later,
a man came into the reception area to greet us.

"Miss Lace?" he asked.

"Yes. This is my friend, Jason Walters," I said as we both stood up to greet him.

"I'm Agent Cooper. Dan Cooper. Please come with me to my office," he said. We followed him down a long corridor to a door marked PRIVATE and entered the large office. There was another man already seated next to the desk.

"This is my partner, Agent Willis," he said. "Tom, this is Devonie Lace, and—I'm sorry, what was your name again?" His brow raised as he looked at Jason.

"Jason Walters," he replied, shaking the man's hand.

"Good to meet you. Now, why don't you tell us what this is all about," Agent Willis said.

I explained my story from the beginning—giving all the details, except for the money. I opened each of the file folders, and handed the clippings to Agent Cooper. Then I laid the mystery box on his desk. "I found this in the safe, but I don't know what it is."

Agent Cooper picked it up, inspecting it briefly. Then he handed it to his partner. "What do you think, Tom? Electronic scrambling device of some sort?"

"Yeah. Probably. We'd have to send it down to the experts, but I'd bet my last paycheck that's what it is."

"What would it be used for?" I asked.

Agent Willis shifted in his chair. He gave his partner an uneasy look. "We've seen a couple of these devices used in the Middle East. Terrorists use them to bring down planes, and sometimes helicopters. They have the ability to cause some of the electronic mechanisms to be inoperative—or worse—to produce erroneous information without the crew realizing it. They're most effective on the global positioning systems. If a plane can't navigate—especially in bad weather conditions, or at night when there's no visibility—it's pretty vulnerable. They're complicated. Not too many people have the skill to build one.''

''Do you suppose that's how he caused the plane crash in Mexico last year?'' I asked, gesturing to the last newspaper clipping Agent Cooper was holding.

''We don't want to jump to any conclusions, Miss Lace. As far as the government is concerned, that incident was nothing more than pilot error. It's possible we may decide to reopen the investigation, if the evidence points us in that direction. For now, we should probably concentrate on your safety. You say that two men visited your boat?'' Agent Cooper asked.

''Yes. That's right.''

''Can you describe them?''

''One was tall and skinny, and wore a ponytail. He's probably got a broken nose now, and a fairly good-sized lump on the side of his head. The other was shorter and stocky, with no hair at all.''

''And you say that Tony Marino was the only other person besides your friend, Joe, who knew you had the gun?'' Agent Willis asked.

''That's right. Even Jason here didn't know until this morning, when he brought me my Jeep.''

''Where are you staying now, Miss Lace?'' Agent Cooper asked.

''I have my boat tied up over at my aunt and uncle's place in Del Mar. They have a private dock. I'm pretty secure there.''

''That's good. We suggest that you remain there until we get to the bottom of this. We'll probably assign an agent to keep an eye on you if we ascertain that your well-being is at risk,'' Agent Cooper explained.

''Do you have any idea how long this will take to clear

up? I mean, how long will I have to stay in hiding? I have to work and earn a living in the meantime.''

''We suggest you don't go to your job for now. Call in sick, or take a vacation. You shouldn't go near any place you regularly hang out. That'll be the first place someone would look for you,'' Agent Cooper explained. ''As far as how long this will take? That's hard to say. It depends on who's behind it all, and how much they want to avoid being caught.''

''Great.'' I sighed. ''I guess I can look for some kind of work in Del Mar in the meantime.''

Agent Willis made some notes in a small notepad. ''Can you give us a number where we can reach you, Miss Lace?''

''Yes. Of course,'' I said, and gave him my cell phone number.

''Thank you, Miss Lace. We'll keep you informed of our investigation. In the meantime, be very careful, and follow our suggestions. Okay?''

''Okay. Thank you both,'' I said. I stood up and walked with Jason toward the door.

I dropped Jason off at his shop. ''Are you going straight back to Del Mar now?'' he asked me.

''No. First I'm going to stop and buy a power cord for the computer. Then I need to pick up groceries and stuff. After that, I'll go back to my . . . my hideout. Doesn't it sound so James Bondish?'' I laughed.

''It's not funny, Dev. You need to be careful.''

The grin left my face. ''I know. I will.''

I called the Grille from the parking lot of the computer supply store to let them know I would not be able to work this weekend. My boss whined that I had just recently taken time off—but I explained that I had a personal emergency, and it couldn't be helped.

By the time I pulled into my aunt and uncle's driveway, it was nearly six o'clock. As I carried the computer and a bag of groceries down the dock, Craig came trotting up behind me. "Wait up, Devonie. Let me help you carry some of that."

"Oh. Hi, Craig. Thanks," I said as I handed him the bag of groceries.

"What's that? A laptop computer?" he asked.

"Yeah. I had to buy a power cord for it today. I picked it up at an auction earlier this week, but the battery is dead."

"Your aunt told me you're into buying and selling stuff like that. Do you make a decent living at it?" he questioned.

"Oh, I get by. Once in a while I make a really good deal. When that happens, I can put a little something into savings. Like last month—I bought this storage unit in San Diego. It was full of all kinds of stuff that looked like junk—to most people. Most of it actually *was* junk. But the guy who had rented it left a bunch of old movie posters behind. They turned out to be collector's items. I found a dealer up in Hollywood who paid me top dollar for them. But that doesn't happen very often."

"How long have you been in this business?" he asked.

"I started about a year ago. I used to be a database administrator, but I discovered that I'm not cut out for the rat race. I had to change my lifestyle, before I became roadkill on the corporate highway. So, here I am."

"I think it's great that you're able to do this. I admire a

person who can take control of their life, and make changes like that.''

''Oh, I don't know how much control I have. I just know life's a lot less stressful now. I feel so much better, it's unbelievable.'' I replayed what I'd just said in my head. I sensed stress would be creeping back into my life big-time—very soon. I only hoped I'd have the strength to handle it better than my history indicated.

''That's great. Hey, I guess I'm having dinner with you all tonight. Your aunt just called and invited me over.''

I laughed. ''She must have waited until she saw me pull into the driveway. I'm sure she's attempting a little match-making. I hope you don't mind.''

''Mind? Are you kidding? I never pass up a chance at a home-cooked meal. At my house, if it doesn't go straight from the freezer to the microwave, it can't be food.''

We both laughed. When we got to the boat, I thanked him for his help. ''You go on ahead. I'll be right up. I just want to put this stuff away. Can you let Aunt Arlene know that I'll be right there?''

''Sure thing,'' he said. He headed back up the dock, toward the house.

I smiled and watched him walk away. He seemed like a really nice man—sort of a Jimmy Stewart–type character. For some reason, I was reminded of the last serious relationship I had with a man. It had ended nearly ten years ago, when my significant other of seven years informed me that he had finally met Miss Right, and she wasn't me. In one cruel instant, I learned a very harsh lesson—not to trust anyone with my heart, unless I was willing to have it broken. I correlate the experience to running headlong into an electric fence, which I had done as a young girl growing up on a small horse ranch. It knocks you flat on your rear, because you don't expect it. Then, every time you come up to any fence, even if you know for a fact that the fence charger is not on, you can't make yourself touch it. I decided a long time ago that no man exists who is worth going through that pain again—although there is a small part of me that hopes I'm wrong.

I dismissed the thoughts, trying to concentrate on putting the groceries away. Finally I sat down at the table with the computer in front of me. I powered the machine up. It prompted me for a password. I guess I shouldn't have been surprised the former owner would have secured the thing. I was sure there were all kinds of incriminating information stored on it. I tried a few things off the top of my head: *spy, killer, assassin,* but of course nothing happened. It was just a shot in the dark, anyway. I shut the machine down, and put it back in the closet. Tomorrow, I could call Spencer, my hacker friend up in Sacramento, and ask for his help. He can break into any computer system you sit him down in front of. He's working for the state now. He was caught adjusting credit card account balances for some of his friends. He was given the choice either to work for the state, in their information technology department, or spend time in the state's own penal "hotel" for several years. Spencer's not stupid. He chose the cushy state position, with all its benefits. (That would be the job, not jail.)

Aunt Arlene made a great dinner. My mouth watered as I smelled the sweet aroma of chopped apples and walnuts being sautéed with tender pieces of chicken breasts, and seasoned with thyme. I helped her halve the avocados she intended to stuff with the chicken mixture. Served over a bed of fresh greens, the meal looked almost too pretty to eat. The deep purple of the cabbage contrasted perfectly with the dark green romaine lettuce and the ripe, red tomatoes. You could have photographed the dinner table to create a perfect still life. Uncle Doug opened a bottle of merlot they picked up in the Napa Valley while on vacation. I couldn't remember the last time I had such a delicious meal. For dessert, we had red raspberry cheesecake. A thin layer of dark chocolate, hidden between the buttery crust and filling, gave my taste buds an enjoyable surprise. Uncle Doug told us it was Aunt Arlene's own creation—called ''Passion in a Pan.''

''Oh, Doug! It is not. I can't believe you said that. Don't you listen to him. He's just trying to embarrass me,'' Arlene defended. Her face blushed a shade almost as red as the raspberry sauce poured over the dessert.

We retired to the living room with our coffee and talked while we admired the sunset on the Pacific. Craig talked about growing up back in Kentucky, and how much he loved the West Coast. He originally planned to return to Kentucky after medical school, to open a practice in the small town he grew up in. Two months before graduation, he took a weekend trip to San Diego, and changed his mind.

''So, Craig . . .'' Aunt Arlene started as she cleared the throw pillows from the love seat to make room for Craig to sit next to me. ''How is it that a nice young man such as yourself isn't married yet?''

Surprised at her directness, Doug decided to come to Craig's rescue by changing the subject before he had a chance to respond. ''Hey, I picked up a great movie at the video place today. You guys want to watch it?'' Uncle Doug asked, eyeing Arlene to be sure she got his drift. ''I think we even have some popcorn.''

''Sure. Sounds great to me,'' I said.

"I'll second that," Craig chimed.

A few silent moments passed, and it seemed Doug had been successful in diverting the direction of the conversation. Then poor Craig put it right back in Aunt Arlene's court. "How is it that I'm still single? Well, I guess I just haven't met the right girl yet. My mother says I'm too picky, but I don't think so. I just have this feeling when I find the right girl, I'll know she's the one, and there won't be any question about it."

"How sweet," Arlene said.

I was silent. I thought to myself, *Poor, naive Craig— he'll be lucky if he even meets Miss Close, let alone Miss Perfect. And then she'll probably tear his heart out. What a cynic I've become.*

It was almost eleven when Craig walked me back to my boat. We laughed together about my aunt's matchmaking attempts. I kept the conversation light, careful to remain within my comfort zone. I thanked him for walking me home, and said good night. It would have felt natural to give him an innocent kiss on the cheek, but that would have been like playing with fire. I sent him on his way, and retired to my little galley.

I tried a couple more times at breaking the password, but was unsuccessful. I finally gave up. I checked my little phone book to make sure I still had Spencer's number.

I changed into the oversize T-shirt I sleep in, and climbed into bed. I was asleep before my head hit the pillow.

I don't remember if I was dreaming at all, but at two in the morning, I woke up suddenly. "That's it," I said as I jumped out of bed. I tried to switch on the light, but nothing happened. I had no power. I grabbed a flashlight and walked outside, to see if the cord had come unplugged from the outlet on the dock. Everything looked okay. I glanced up at the house, and saw the porch lights on. The breaker must have needed to be reset, I thought to myself, but I didn't know where it was. I could ask Uncle Doug to show me in the morning. For now, I needed to plug in the computer and try something. I slipped on some jeans and a sweatshirt and deck shoes. I grabbed the laptop, and carried it up to the house. I plugged it into an electrical outlet located near the picnic table where I sat down. I booted the little machine up, and waited for the password prompt. I said a little prayer, then typed in the name *Kerstin.*

"Yes," I whispered, as the Windows 95 desktop appeared before my eyes. I started moving the mouse pointer to the Windows Explorer button when it happened.

At first, I thought the sound came from out on the open ocean, not the confines of the small harbor. You just wouldn't expect something with an impact that immense to happen so close. The explosion was massive. The sound would have ousted the entire neighborhood from their beds. My attention was redirected away from the small screen of the computer, to the inferno blazing in the harbor. For a brief moment, I thought this must be one more of my crazy dreams—only it seemed much more realistic than usual. I blinked my eyes several times to confirm I was, in fact, awake and what I was seeing was reality. My beautiful boat had gone up in a mass of flames. Debris flew through the air like little missiles. The explosion destroyed half the dock, along with the *Plan B.* I sat in a daze as I watched my home burning like a torch.

Seconds later, Doug and Arlene came running out of the

house to see what the blast was. "Devonie! Your boat blew up!" Uncle Doug exclaimed, in shock.

I didn't take my eyes off the flames. "I know, Uncle Doug. I know."

Chapter Ten

I took a quick mental inventory of all my belongings, and where they were. Of course, almost everything I owned was on the boat. Basically, all I had left were the clothes I was wearing, the computer I was sitting in front of, and my Jeep. The Jeep was going to be completely useless to me at the moment. The keys, along with all my credit cards, driver's license, and any other forms of ID I had, were in my purse. The last place I recalled seeing my purse was on the table in the galley of the *Plan B*.

"Thank heavens you weren't on the boat. Are you okay, Devonie? Oh, my. I'd better go call the fire department. Are you sure you're all right? What in the world happened?" Aunt Arlene gushed.

"Calm down, honey," Doug said, in the most composed voice he could muster under the circumstances. "You go call 911. I'll try to find out what happened."

The situation grew more intense by the moment. Neighbors bolted from their homes to see what all the commotion was about. Dogs barked furiously at small pieces of burning debris landing in their yards.

"Uncle Doug, I think I need some help," I said as I frantically packed the computer back in its case.

"It looks like Pearl Harbor out there. What's going on, Devonie? What happened to your boat?" he demanded.

"I can't explain everything right now. I don't have time. I need to get out of here before the fire department and police show up. In a nutshell, I bought the contents of a storage unit that apparently belonged to some sort of assassin. Besides some pretty powerful weaponry, I acquired a rather large sum of money. Somehow, someone found out that I have the stuff, and now I guess they want to kill me. That's why I came here—to hide—because I found out they were after me. I don't know how in the world they found me here, but it's obvious they know where I am. I tried to turn on the lights on the boat, but there was no power. It's just a miracle I came up here to find a plug at the very moment the boat went up. Someone up there must be watching over me."

"That circuit breaker must have blown again. I've been meaning to have an electrician come look at it. Anyhow, that's beside the point. The lucky thing is that you're still alive. It sounds like you'd be safer if everyone else thinks you went up with your boat, though."

"Exactly. But I've got to move fast. I think I should get away from here as soon as possible, in case they come back to make sure they were successful. I can't use my Jeep because I don't have the keys. . . . Wait. The spare set Jason used to bring it to me . . . I think I left those on the desk in your study."

"You may have, but you shouldn't use your Jeep. They

probably know it's yours and they might be looking for it. You can use one of my company cars in the meantime. I've got a company credit card for a new salesman who's starting next week. You can use it, and no one will be able to trace it back to you. I'll let everyone believe that you were on the boat. Of course, I imagine when they start searching for your remains and can't find them, they'll come to some conclusions.''

''You're probably right, but at least it may buy me some time. I've been in contact with the FBI. As soon as I get relocated, I'll call the agent I talked to today. I'm sure they'll offer me some protection.''

''That's a good idea, Devonie. Just give me a minute to get that credit card from my desk. I'll meet you at the big garage.''

I spotted Craig jogging across the immense grassy area that separated his home from Doug and Arlene's. I quickly ducked into the shadows of some large decorative bushes. I wanted to avoid being spotted by him, or anyone else who might recognize me as the nice young woman who owned the boat that just blew up. I quietly made my way along the wall to the corner of the house. The ''big'' garage, as Uncle Doug called it, was a meticulously kept storage building for his impressive collection of classic and sports cars. The everyday automobiles were kept in a standard two-car garage attached to the house, but the big garage was a detached building about one hundred feet away, on the other side of the driveway. I couldn't see a way to get from the house to the garage without being totally exposed. I briefly scanned the area, checking for anyone who might be looking in my direction. Once he realized it was my boat on fire, Craig broke into a full run toward the dock. He was obviously concerned, and part of me wanted to call out to him to let him know I was all right. But I thought better of it. This was no time to let my heart take control over my head. I made a mad dash across the brick driveway, and back into the shadows of the impressive building, designed to match the stately home it accompanied.

Uncle Doug was opening the last of three automatic garage doors. "There you are, Devonie. Take your pick," he said as he motioned to his collection of company cars. Parked there in the meticulously attired garage was a Testarossa, a metallic silver-blue BMW Z3 roadster, and a deep forest green Jaguar E-type convertible.

"Gee, Uncle Doug. Which one do you think will be the least conspicuous?" I jested.

"I'd go for the Ferrari myself, but I believe the BMW would suit you better."

"Okay. Then the BMW it is," I said as he handed me the keys.

"Now, the tank is full and there's a car phone in the jockey box. Here's a credit card for gas and lodging and whatever else you might need. You be careful, and call us as soon as you can."

"I will, Uncle Doug. Thank you so much."

I put the computer on the passenger seat next to me, and started the engine. I eased down the long dark driveway with my headlights off, until I pulled onto the main thoroughfare. I passed a parade of fire trucks, police cars, and an ambulance. The flashing red lights blinded me as they passed. I cringed at the blaring sound of the sirens as they hurled past my little roadster. I watched in the rearview mirror as they all turned onto the drive I had just come from. I went through the gears and sped off into the darkness, not sure where I was going. I finally decided to head north. I found a small, out-of-the-way motel in San Clemente, and checked in. Exhausted, I decided to try to get some sleep before the sun came up.

Morning came too soon. I tried to focus my eyes on the small blue numbers on the digital clock next to the bed. I think it said seven-thirty, but everything was still a little fuzzy. I dragged myself into the bathroom and splashed some water on my face. I decided to call Jason first, to let him know what happened. I didn't want him to see it on the five o'clock news and think I was dead. I picked up the phone and dialed his number. A woman answered the phone.

"Oh gosh. I'm sorry it's so early. I think I have the wrong number," I apologized, ready to hang up.

"Are you calling for Jason?" the woman asked.

I hesitated. Jason hadn't told me about any relationships he was in at the moment, and I wondered who this woman might be. "Well, yes, actually. Is he there?"

The woman's weak voice cracked and wavered. She sounded as though she hadn't slept in days. "Jason was in a serious car accident last night. He's in the hospital. Are you a friend of his?" she asked.

"Yes, I am. Is he okay?" I asked, shocked at the news.

"Well, he's in a coma right now. The doctors aren't sure . . . aren't sure he's going to make it," she bawled. Once she regained her composure, she continued. "I'm his sister, Jennifer. My mother and I just came over to get a few of his things, in case he wakes up. We're trying to stay positive."

"What hospital is he in?" I asked.

"He's at San Diego General. He's still in intensive care, so there's no room number yet."

"Do you know how the accident happened?" I asked.

"The highway patrolman said it was a single-car accident. Apparently, he was speeding when he lost control and drove off the embankment. It was quite a drop. He's lucky to be alive.'' She sniffed and excused herself momentarily so she could blow her nose into a Kleenex. ''If he wakes up, who can I tell him called?''

''I'm just a friend from his shop. You have enough to worry about without having to keep track of messages for him. I'll keep checking with the hospital to see how he's doing. You just take care of him . . . and make sure they're doing everything possible.''

''Oh, believe me. We are.''

I set the receiver back in its cradle, and stared at the phone. I picked it up again and started to dial the FBI. I got the first four digits dialed when I stopped and hung up. Jason was not a radical driver. If anything, he was too cautious behind the wheel. I used to call him Grandpa whenever I rode with him, because he drove so slowly. I knew that he didn't just lose control and drive off a cliff without some help. My mind raced through a dozen possible scenarios. The only people who knew anything about Jason's involvement with me—and the assassin's belongings— were the FBI. Unless someone followed him from the marina when he brought me the Jeep. How could I be sure?

I powered up the computer again. I'd never had a chance to check it out last night before the explosion. There were the usual shortcuts on the desktop. There were also a couple of items I didn't recognize. There was an icon for something called VideoService. It sounded like some sort of movie club. I wondered if Mr. Kephart was into some kind of kinky stuff. I decided it wasn't worth investigating. I navigated to the My Documents directory to search for anything that might be of some assistance. The directory was totally empty. I checked other directories, in case he had decided to use his own filing conventions, but found nothing. I started to think there was nothing on this machine that would help me at all. I opened up Microsoft Exchange and browsed the in-box. It was empty. Mr. Kephart was very careful about cleaning up his E-mail. At least, I'm sure he thought he was careful. I navigated to his deleted-items directory. Pay dirt. Apparently, nobody ever explained to him that deleted items aren't truly deleted until they are physically removed—unless the defaults are set to automatically remove them upon leaving the system. I opened the first file. The screen came up with the photos of two men—David Powers and Michael Norris. These were the two men killed in the plane crash. The text of the document read:

Mr. Kephart,

These two men are agents for the DEA. They are currently involved in an investigation that will take them to Guadalajara city in Mexico during the first weeks of July. They are working in cooperation with Mexico's Federal Judicial Police to shut down the largest drug trafficking operation in Mexico. It is vital that they do not return to the United States and continue with this investigation. Do whatever is necessary to prevent their return and prevent them from having any *contact with* any *officials* anywhere *in the world. In other words, Mr. Kephart, these two men must be eliminated. It is vital that whatever happens to them appears accidental. We do not want any speculation into the cause of their deaths. Per your instructions, we have deposited five hundred thousand dollars into the specified account in Geneva. The remainder of the payment will be delivered to you after the assignment*

*is completed. Your reputation precedes you, and I am
sure that I can count on your complete and total dis-
cretion in this matter.*

The sender of this document was identified only as CH.
Could that be the "Carl H" name I tried to read on the
notepad from the briefcase? Who was this "Carl H," and
what reason could he have for wanting the two men dead?
What could his connection be with the Mexican drug
operation?

The next file was also from CH. The first page looked
like an excerpt from an official FAA report on the plane
crash that killed the two DEA agents. It described an unidentified electronic box found in the wreckage that was
apparently stowed in the baggage compartment of the
plane. The report was signed by the official FAA investigator, and his card, with his office address and phone number, was copied in the corner. The next page was brief and
to the point:

Mr. Kephart,

*This would appear to be a messy detail. I thought
I made it clear that there should be no reason for
speculation into this matter. I have been forced to use
my own resources to take care of this potentially dis-
astrous mistake. Of course, there will be an adjustment
to your final payment, to reflect my dissatisfaction with
your work. You can be assured, if any investigation
comes of this, and I am involved in any way, your fate
will be as bleak as that of Powers and Norris. I made
an oath to myself when I took this position—I will
never go down alone. I will take down as many*

people with me as I can possibly name, and you are no exception.

There were no other items of importance in the deleted-items directory. I picked up the phone and dialed the number of the FAA investigator identified on the report.

"Hello. May I speak with Mr. Frank Eastwood, please?" I requested.

"Oh. I'm sorry. Mr. Eastwood is no longer with us," came the reply.

"He isn't? May I ask how I can reach him?"

"Well, I guess you could try a séance—Frank passed away about a year ago."

"Oh. I'm sorry to hear that. How did it happen?"

"He and his wife were killed in a plane crash—very tragic."

How ironic, I thought to myself. "Was it a commercial airline?" I asked.

"No. Frank loved to fly in his free time. He had a nice Thorp T-18. He built it himself. He and his wife were taking a trip to Alaska when they went down in some pretty rugged terrain. His last radio transmission was very grim. He lost his oil pressure—engine quit with nothing for miles but mountains and trees. Never found them or the plane, but there's no chance they survived up there. Searchers looked for weeks. Poor Frank. He was such a good guy, too. We really miss him around here."

"Well, I'm sorry I had to bring it all up again. Thank you for your time. Good-bye."

I made one more call. I didn't want to be too specific over the phone—in case anyone was listening in on the conversation. "Uncle Doug. Can you meet me for lunch at that place you and Aunt Arlene took me for my thirteenth birthday?''

He hesitated for a moment—trying to remember back that far, I guess. ''Oh. Sure. I'll meet you out front at noon. Are you okay?''

''I'm fine. I'll see you at twelve. 'Bye.''

I stopped to pick up a battery for the laptop and a box of diskettes on my way back to San Diego. I sat in the car in the parking lot and made several backup copies of the E-mail documents Robert Kephart had left on his computer. A man's voice startled me while I waited for the last copy to be made.

''Nice car,'' he said as he leaned over the passenger side door, admiring the sports car. He hid his face behind a pair of dark reflective sunglasses that looked as if they came right out of the seventies. He wore a pair of jeans about as tight as the casing of an overstuffed Polish sausage. His dark shirt was unbuttoned halfway down, exposing a collection of gold chains that would put Mr. T to shame. On his right hand was a hideously gaudy piece of oversize gold jewelry. On his other hand, believe it or not, he wore a mood ring. I hadn't seen one of those since high school. He also sported a pair of pointy, high-heeled alligator-skin cowboy boots, complete with sterling-silver toe caps. To top off the entire ensemble, he wore a black mohair cowboy hat with a Confederate flag pinned to the front of it. He reeked of Calvin Klein's Eternity for Men, a scent that I used to find very appealing—at least up until that moment.

''Thank you,'' I said, not offering any other words to encourage a conversation. He gave me the creeps, and I wanted him to be on his way.

''It's a BMW. Right?''

''That's right. A Z3 roadster,'' I replied.

''Like the one in the James Bond movie, huh?''

''Yeah. I think so.''

''Cool,'' he said as he stepped back to admire the body of the car. ''Think I could take her for a spin?''

I laughed. ''You're kidding. Right?''

''No way. I'd be careful. Just once around the block?''

''I don't think so. I'm late for an appointment,'' I said, and started the engine. As I backed out of the parking spot, I watched him walk to his car—an older model bright-yellow Porsche Targa. He followed me out of the parking lot. He tailgated me all the way to the highway.

''Oh great,'' I said to myself. ''All I need is for this guy to pester me all the way to San Diego.''

I made several turns to try to lose him, but he kept right on my tail. I picked up speed, and started weaving in and out of traffic. When I thought I had lost him, I quickly darted into the parking lot of a small restaurant. I parked in the back so the car wouldn't be visible from the road. I went inside for a few minutes to give the jerk time to get out of the vicinity.

I sat in a booth with my iced tea, and watched a brother and sister torment each other in the booth next to mine. He would pull her hair, and she would punch him in the arm. The parents would make promises of punishment, but the threats were useless. The mother left the booth to make a phone call, and the father went to the rest room. Then I watched in amazement as the boy took the wad of gum he was chewing on, and dropped it in the fresh bottle of ketchup the waitress had placed on their table. He used a straw to push it just beneath the surface, so it wasn't visible. The two little brats squealed with delight at the ingenious act. Suddenly, they were the best of friends. When their parents returned, the happy family packed themselves up in the minivan, and were on their way.

It wasn't until then that I noticed the jerk in the yellow Porsche. He had somehow slithered in and taken the booth behind me, without me noticing him. He must have checked every parking lot on the street, looking for the Z3. This guy was some sort of crazy stalker. When I turned and noticed him, he smiled and waved, like we were old friends. He ordered a burger and fries, and rudely interrupted the busy waitress, demanding ketchup.

I smiled, got up from my table, and picked up the bottle of Heinz from the little urchins' booth. I strolled over to his table, and placed it in front of him. "Here you go," I said politely. Then I whispered "Bozo" to myself as I turned and walked away.

I paid my bill, and quickly left. As much as I wanted to stick around and watch the expression on his face when he bit into the big wad of Bazooka bubble gum in his hamburger, I decided it would be wiser for me to be on my way. As I pulled out of the parking lot, he came running out of the restaurant, cursing at me.

I stuck my foot onto the accelerator, and squealed around the corner. That darn little yellow Porsche was on my tail before I knew it. I was speeding dangerously through traffic, trying to locate a freeway on-ramp. He just stuck to me like glue. I glanced over my shoulder, to see if I could change lanes. No open spot. I swerved into the oncoming traffic lane. I checked my speedometer—seventy-five miles per hour. The speed limit sign read thirty-five. I dashed back into my own lane just in time to escape a head-on with a Cadillac. A short break in the oncoming traffic gave me an opportunity to get off the Pacific Coast Highway. I squealed left, through a red light, and onto a small side street. My yellow shadow haunted me. I couldn't seem to lose him. Racing through a quiet residential area, we must have looked like a couple of Grand Prix wanna-bes.

Suddenly, a small calico cat, carrying a kitten in her mouth, trotted out in front of me. I slammed the brakes on. The Porsche squealed to a halt behind me, coming to within one inch of my bumper. Mama kitty, startled by the commotion, stopped dead in her tracks in panic. She dashed left, then right, then left again. I watched in my rearview mirror as the driver-side door of the Porsche opened. Finally, the feline came to her senses, and carried her baby to the safety of a large planter box in the next yard. Just as my pursuer reached the rear fender, I punched the accelerator, and sped off. He jumped back into his little bumblebee car, and resumed the chase.

Somehow, I found myself back on the main highway, only this time, heading north. I just couldn't seem to lose him. Then, all of a sudden, he disappeared. Soon enough, I realized why.

When I saw the flashing red lights and heard the siren, my heart sank. I pulled over and sat helplessly as I waited for my fate to be dished out to me. The little yellow Porsche raced by, and honked his horn as he passed. What a jerk.

"May I see your license and registration, please?" the officer asked.

"I'm sorry, but I don't have my license with me. I seem to have lost it," I confessed. "But here's the registration," I said as I rummaged through the glove box, searching for the certificate.

He inspected the registration certificate. "Are you an employee of Douglas Lace Yacht Brokerage?" he asked.

"No. Douglas Lace is my uncle. He loaned me this car."

"I see. What's your name?" he asked.

"Devonie Lace."

"Do you have any identification?"

"Well, not actually, officer."

He eyed me suspiciously. "May I ask why you don't have any ID?"

I bit my lip and hesitated, trying to think of a good excuse. Sympathy seemed to be my best shot in a situation like this. "Well, you see, I had this fight with my boyfriend last night. He took me out to dinner at the Pier Restaurant. After dinner, we walked out to the end of the pier, and he said he had something very important to ask me. I thought for sure he was going to propose, since we've been dating for nearly seven years now. I had told him that I wasn't going to wait much longer for him to make up his mind. Anyhow, he didn't propose. He asked if I could loan him twelve hundred dollars for one of his crazy, get-rich-quick schemes—that never materialize. I told him no, and that I never wanted to see him again. After all, he never repaid me from all the other times I loaned him money and he promised to pay me back." I mustered up all the emotion I could, and even managed a tear or two. "Anyhow, he grabbed my purse and we struggled over it." I paused to wipe the tears from my face.

The officer seemed sympathetic. "So, he stole your purse?" he asked.

"Not exactly. I wouldn't let that little weasel have it. I grabbed it back and swung it at him. I missed and it slipped out of my hands—flew right out into the water."

He shook his head and smiled. "I see," he said.

* * *

"Hello. Uncle Doug?"

"Devonie? Where are you?" he blurted.

"There's been a slight change in our lunch plans. Can you meet me at the San Clemente police station instead?"

Chapter Eleven

The police station was a pretty quiet place. Apparently, there wasn't a lot of crime going on there. I sat in an overstuffed chair that swiveled and rocked, while I waited for Uncle Doug to arrive to verify my identity. The officers were very nice, offering me pastries and cappuccino. I fidgeted with a puzzle sitting on the desk nearest me. Finally, a familiar face came through the automatic sliding-glass doors.

"Uncle Doug. Boy, am I glad to see you. I was afraid they were going to lock me up pretty soon."

"No way I'd let that happen. Now, where's the idiot I need to see to straighten out this mess?"

"He's right over there," I said as I pointed to the officer who brought me in. "Hey, Bruce. My uncle is here."

The officer put down a file he was reading, and walked over to us. "How do you do, sir? I'm Officer Mahoney. I understand you may be able to clear up a little confusion for us regarding your niece.''

"What's the confusion here? My name is Douglas Lace, and this is my niece, Devonie Lace. I loaned her one of my company cars, and the next thing I know, some bozo has hauled her in here for some ridiculously lame reason.''

"Now, take it easy, Uncle Doug. They've been very nice to me here. Don't get so excited,'' I said, trying to keep things from heating up.

"Nice? You think hauling you in here and towing my car is a nice thing to do?''

Officer Mahoney interrupted. "Now, Mr. Lace. You have to look at the situation objectively. Your niece was speeding when I stopped her. She had no identification at all, and she was driving a very expensive sports car that didn't belong to her. Under the circumstances, I had no choice but to bring her down to the station, until we could contact the owner of the car to verify it wasn't stolen. I'm sure if the situation were different, and your car *had* been stolen, you would appreciate our caution.''

Uncle Doug thought about it for a moment, then nodded his head in agreement. "Yes. I suppose you're right. Anyhow, what do we need to do to get my little Devonie out of here? She has important appointments to keep, I'm sure.''

"As long as you can show proof that you own the car, then your niece is free to go, Mr. Lace.''

After clearing everything up, I thanked Bruce for the pastries, and walked with Uncle Doug out to the corridor. "I'm going to use the ladies' room. I'll meet you in the parking lot. Okay?'' I said.

"Okay.''

I washed and dried my hands, and inspected my face in

the mirror. *I could use some makeup,* I thought to myself as I tried to fluff some life into my exhausted hair and pinch some color into my pale cheeks. The next chance I got, I would have to stop and get some basic toiletries. I pushed through the rest-room door and made my way through the maze of hallways toward the exit.

I stopped dead in my tracks when I saw the two men. I quickly ducked around a corner to avoid being seen. It was Cooper and Willis, the FBI agents I had spoken to before my boat blew up. What were they doing here? Could they be looking for me? How could they have found out I was here so quickly? What a silly question. This was the FBI I was dealing with. Their resources were probably unlimited, when it came to getting information about everyday citizens like me. I waited very quietly, and tried to listen to their conversation, but I couldn't make out what they were saying. Then I heard their footsteps behind me. They got closer. I panicked. There was nowhere to hide. If they came down this hallway, I'd be a sitting duck. I backed up tightly against the wall, and didn't make a move. My heart pounded so loudly, I thought everyone in the building could hear it. Beads of sweat rolled down the sides of my face. My knees weakened, and I felt certain I was going to slide right down the wall onto the floor. I held my breath as they passed the corridor, never even turning a glance at me. I breathed a sigh of relief as they disappeared around the corner, out of sight. I collected myself as best I could, and hurried out of the building. I found Uncle Doug waiting by his car.

"I've got to get out of here right away, Uncle Doug. I don't have time to explain. Can you meet me at my bank in an hour? Do you remember where it is—where we signed all the papers when I bought the *Plan B*?"

"I remember. I'll see you in an hour. Now, get going."

I found the BMW parked in a small lot next to the station. I started the engine, and carefully pulled onto the main street. I kept checking my rearview mirror. The only car following me was Uncle Doug's, as far as I could tell. I made my way to the freeway, and headed south—back toward San Diego. The traffic was heavy—typical for this time of day. I was careful to maintain the posted speed limit. I didn't need any more complications today.

I parked in front of the bank, and Uncle Doug pulled in right next to me. "Uncle Doug, I've got to get into my safe-deposit box. Do you have any idea how I can do that without the key, or any identification to prove who I am?"

"The manager here is a friend of mine. I just let him beat me at a game of golf Saturday. My company brings a lot of business to him. He should be able to do me a favor."

"I hope so. I've got to get into that box." I moaned in frustration.

"Well, let's go inside, and see if he's even here today." I followed him through the bank doors.

"Good day. Is Harvey Champion in today?" he asked the woman at the counter.

"He is," she answered.

"I wonder if you could tell him Doug Lace is here to see him? It's rather urgent."

"Certainly. Please wait here, Mr. Lace," she said, then disappeared through a door marked PRIVATE.

She returned a few moments later, with the bank manager following her. "Doug. How are you doing? Still recovering from that beating I gave you on the course Saturday?"

"You bet, Harv. You're going to have to give me some pointers on my game, before we play again." Uncle Doug gave me a wink. He once told me he never allowed himself to beat a prospective client, or banker, at golf. It was one of his business rules. Today, I saw why he made that rule.

"Anytime, old buddy. Now, what can I do for you?" he asked.

"This is my niece, Devonie. Can we go into your office, Harv? We have a favor to discuss with you."

"Sure thing, Doug. Just come right around here, and follow me," he said as he motioned to a small gate at the end of the counter. We followed him to his office and sat in some very unattractive, contemporary-style chairs that were about as uncomfortable as they were ugly.

Uncle Doug explained that all my belongings had been destroyed in a fire, and that I needed to get into my safe-deposit box.

Harvey peered at me over his glasses. "You don't have the key?" he asked.

"No. It was lost in the explosion," I explained.

"And you don't have any ID at all?" he questioned.

"Well, my passport is in the safe-deposit box. I could show it to you, if you can let me into it."

A very cautious man, Harvey carefully contemplated what we asked of him. With the current trends in downsizing, he would not likely take any risks that might jeopardize his position. But on the other hand, Uncle Doug had brought millions of dollars' worth of business to this bank, and Harvey knew that he could just as easily do business elsewhere.

"I'm going to do it for you, Doug, but it is highly irregular. Please keep this to yourselves. Okay?"

"Thanks, Harv. I owe you one," Uncle Doug promised.

"Yes. Thank you, Mr. Champion. You may just be saving my life."

He smiled at me, not realizing I was totally serious. "Okay. Let's go get you into that box."

I rummaged through my personal papers. I found the ownership documents for the *Plan B,* and the pink slip for my Jeep. There were insurance policies, and my birth certificate. Finally, I found my passport, and laid it on the table. Then I got the briefcase out and untaped it. I gazed at the rows of money and thought for a moment. I reached in and took out one bundle. I lowered the lid to the case, and retaped it closed. I tucked the bundle of money inside my waistband, and hoped it didn't look too conspicuous. Luckily, my sweatshirt was large, and my lopsidedness wasn't noticeable.

I showed Harvey my passport, and he seemed relieved. He was comforted with the fact that he had helped another human being, and that he would probably still have a job tomorrow.

Uncle Doug and I walked back to the parking lot. I pulled the bundle out from under my sweatshirt. Then, I extracted about half of the bills from the wad, and handed them to my uncle. "I want you to take this. I know you lost half of your dock when my boat blew up. I'm really sorry for all the trouble I've brought you and Aunt Arlene. I don't know if this is enough to rebuild your dock, but there's more if it isn't."

"Now, wait a minute, Devonie. You know I have insurance to cover that. You don't need to do this," he insisted, as he tried to force the money back into my hand.

"No. Now, I know your insurance company will balk when they discover the boat was intentionally destroyed, and you may have trouble getting them to pay. Just take this, and use it. The money is probably from the people who destroyed the dock in the first place. It's only fair that they pay to repair it.''

He could see I was not going to give in on this, so he reluctantly put the money into his jacket pocket. ''You are just as hardheaded as my brother. I'm sure glad I didn't inherit that trait.''

I laughed.

''Now, what's going on? Who are you running from?''

''The FBI.''

''What?''

''Uncle Doug. This thing goes way deeper than I ever imagined. I think my little escapade at the San Clemente police station probably tipped off the FBI that I wasn't on the boat when she went up.'' I opened the glove box of the BMW, and took out one of the floppy disk copies I had made earlier, and handed it to him. ''Do you still have that friend who works at the *Los Angeles Times*?'' I asked.

''Yes. Why?''

''Take a look at what's on this disk. It may explain some of what's going on. Then send it to your friend. He probably won't do anything with it without any substantiation, but if something happens to me, someone down there may decide to do some investigating.''

''Devonie. I don't like this. This is looking way too dangerous.''

''I don't like it either, but I don't know who I can turn to. I have something of a plan, but I need you to take me to the airport. Can you do that?''

''Sure, I can take you. That might not be a bad idea for you to get away from here. Where are you going?''

''I can't say, just yet. Anyway, you'll be safer if you don't know.''

I grabbed the laptop, and we left the BMW parked in

front of the bank. Uncle Doug would pick it up later—after I was safely off. I made him drop me at the unloading zone, and wouldn't let him come in with me.

The flight from San Diego to Los Angeles was short, and about as pleasant as a ride on an overcrowded school bus. I sat in coach, in the middle of a class of sixth- or seventh-grade kids, on their way to some sort of soccer camp. They were all keyed up, and very excited about wherever it was they were headed. I was knocked in the head no less than three times, when the boys seated next to and behind me exchanged sports equipment. Obviously, there wasn't enough adult supervision to keep them under control. When we landed at Los Angeles International, the pilot actually stopped the plane just off the runway, and announced that he would not move the plane another inch until someone got them to sit down and behave.

I presented my passport at the ticket counter, and paid for my ticket with cash. Suddenly, I flashed back to the flight I had just come in on. "How much extra would that be for first class?" I inquired.

"Oh. It's quite a bit more. Just let me check that for you," the ticket agent replied, as she punched some keys on the computer.

My mouth must have fallen open when she told me the fare. I pondered the idea for a moment, then I unfolded the wad of bills again. "Go ahead and make that a first-class ticket."

"Most certainly," she replied, as she took back the documents she had just handed me. Finally, all ticketing procedures were complete.

"Do you have any luggage to check?" she asked.

"No luggage. Just me," I answered.

She gave me a second look, as if she hadn't heard me clearly the first time. "No luggage?"

"No. I'll do some shopping when I get there," I said as I tucked the bundle of bills back under my sweatshirt.

"I see. Well, you have a very pleasant trip, Miss Lace, and please fly with us again," she said, smiling.

"Thank you," I replied, and turned to leave the counter.

I crashed into the man, causing him to drop his carry-on bag.

"Devonie. It *is* you. I thought—"

"Craig. Imagine bumping into you here," I replied. I frantically tried to think of some way to explain how I was still alive, after everyone believed I had been killed on the boat.

"I thought you were dead. *Everyone* thinks you're dead. Your poor aunt and uncle are beside themselves. What the heck is going on?"

I took him by the arm, and shuffled us into a small airport café. I found a quiet table in the corner. "Listen, Craig. It's all too complicated to explain. You just have to believe me when I tell you, if you let anyone know you've seen me, I won't be alive for much longer."

"What's going on, Devonie? What have you gotten yourself into? You need some help."

"No. I don't want you to get involved—you'll only put yourself in danger. Now, please. Just don't tell anyone you've seen me. I've got to go. My flight will be boarding soon."

I started to get up from the table when suddenly, a horrible thought came to my mind. "Oh, no!" I gasped, and collapsed hard, back down in the chair. "Craig. There *is* something you can do for me. There's a patient in the intensive-care unit at San Diego General. His name is Jason

Walters. He was in a car accident, but it wasn't really an accident. Someone forced him off the road. When they find out he survived, I'm sure they'll try to finish him off, before he regains consciousness.''

He stared at me, without saying a word. He studied my face as intensely as a Doberman guard dog confronted with an unexpected stranger. The desperation must have shown in my eyes. I imagine he was trying to decide if I was making this crazy story up, or if it could possibly be true. He must have come to some conclusion, finally. ''That's no problem. I'll just have the police set up a twenty-four-hour watch on him.''

''No. You don't understand. I'm fairly certain the authorities tried to have him killed in the first place—the same people who blew up my boat. Can you put some people you know and trust on a twenty-four-hour watch over him? I'll pay for any expenses. You just tell me how much private nurses cost,'' I said as I pulled the money from my sweatshirt again.

''Keep your money, Devonie. I know some people who can help out. I'll do what I can. You say his name is Jason Walters?''

''Yes. Thank you, Craig. You don't know how much I appreciate this. Now, I've got to go, or I'll miss my flight.''

''Where are you going?'' he asked.

''I can't tell you, Craig. Please, just forget you even saw me today. If anyone asks, you never saw me, and you don't know where I am. I've got to go,'' I said, and hurried out of the café toward my gate.

The flight attendant demonstrated all the emergency procedures as we pulled away from the gate. I stretched out in my first-class seat, and closed my eyes. I needed to think, but I was exhausted. The last thing I remember before falling asleep was the pilot announcing the current temperature in Geneva, over the intercom.

Chapter Twelve

Robert Kephart sat quietly in his hotel room, reading his E-mail again. He had already read it three times. He was troubled, and the effects of having no sleep for days showed on his face. When the phone rang, it startled him. He jumped to grab the receiver, and nearly knocked the laptop computer off the table.

"Yeah," he answered abruptly.

"Kephart?" Carl Hobson's voice asked over the phone line.

"Yeah," he repeated.

"Listen carefully. I have a room at the Marriott. It's number four thirty-four. Be there—alone—in exactly thirty minutes. I've decided to pay you our original agreed-upon price, since it looks like we've taken care of our small FAA problem. But don't expect to get any more business from us in the future. We can't afford screwups like the one you pulled.''

"I'll be there," Robert replied, and hung up the phone. He was still uneasy. This wasn't the usual small-time mobster he was dealing with. This was the CIA, and they could make him disappear, without a trace, in the blink of an eye. He checked his watch. He would just barely have time to get to the Marriott by noon. He deleted the E-mail messages from Hobson, shut down the computer, and packed it up in its case. He cautiously checked for anyone suspicious in the hall before he let himself out of his room. He felt like a sitting duck during hunting season. Hobson was impatiently waiting for him when he knocked on the hotel door.

"I told you noon. I was just about to forget it, and let you settle for only half the payment you've already gotten," Hobson scolded.

"Traffic was bad, and parking was worse," Kephart replied.

"Whatever. Anyhow, here it is," he said as he handed Robert a nylon sports bag. "I don't want to hear from you ever again. If I decide we can do business in the future, I'll contact you. Do you understand?"

"Perfectly," Robert replied, taking the sack from Hobson.

Robert turned to leave the room. Then he looked down at the sack, wondering if it was safe to open. It could be a bomb, for all he knew.

"Wait a minute, Hobson. Mind if we open this together—to make sure the contract is complete?"

Hobson stared at him in disbelief. Then he laughed. "You pathetic loser. You think it's a setup, don't you? Go ahead. Open it, right here."

Robert eyed him suspiciously as he unzipped the bag. Inside were bundles of money. He reached in and inspected one of the bundles. Everything appeared okay. "Looks like you've met your end of the agreement," Robert said as he closed the bag.

Hobson glared at him, then motioned for him to leave. Robert returned to his car, and looked around for any familiar vehicles. He thought he'd sensed someone following him the past couple of days. He drove directly to A-1 Mini Storage, and proceeded to the unit he had recently rented. He transferred the money from the sack to his briefcase, and laid the computer on top of the file cabinet. He had rented this unit and moved out of his furnished apartment when he received the E-mail message from Hobson, expressing his dissatisfaction in the DEA agent job. Kephart decided that relocating his business out of the country would be better for him. Too many people knew how to find him here. He locked the unit up, and went back to his hotel.

Kephart pulled a card out of his pocket, and dialed the number written on it.

"Hello," the gruff voice on the other end answered.

"Khan. It's Kephart."

"Where's my money, Kephart?" Khan demanded.

"Don't worry. I've got your money, you moron. I should keep it, after the mess you've made of this job. You were supposed to take care of that plane remotely, you idiot. What the devil is that box they found in the wreckage?"

Khan didn't answer. He cleared his throat, and restated his question. "Where's my money, Kephart?"

"You'll get your money. You stupid . . . Oh, forget it, you're not worth the aggravation." Kephart paused and thought for a moment. He came to some sort of last-minute decision. "Listen. Just meet me at the airport in front of the United terminal, in two hours. I'll have your money for you. Then you can be on your way to whatever rock you came out from under."

Click. Khan hung up on him. Kephart stared at the receiver in disbelief, then laid it back in its cradle. He picked it up again, and dialed.

"Hello. Kerstin?"

"Yes, Robert. Is that you?" she asked. Her voice sounded anxious, even though he had woken her from a sound sleep.

"It's me. Listen, darling. There's been some trouble with my new business partner. I've just decided I'm going to try to catch a flight out of here tonight, to Geneva. I'm probably going to be staying in Europe for a while. Can you arrange for an apartment for me there? I'll need something with space for an office, and reliable phone service."

"Of course, Robert. Are you okay? You sound strange."

"I'm fine, darling. I just need to get out of here for a while. I'll call you when I arrive in Geneva."

"Okay, Robert. I'll take care of everything here for you."

"Thanks, darling. See you soon."

" 'Bye, Robert," she said, and hung up the phone.

Robert packed the few belongings he had with him, and returned to his car. He would stop at the mini storage unit one more time to pick up the money, and his computer. Before he could get the door unlocked, two men startled him from behind. When he saw them earlier, in the parking garage, he wasn't too concerned. They were both in blue jeans and casual shirts. One wore a San Francisco Giants baseball cap, and the other had a portable radio, with the headphones draped loosely around his neck. It appeared as if they were on their way to a baseball game. Robert, of all people, should have realized how looks could be deceiving. In an instant, the one with the cap was pressing the barrel of a gun in his back.

"Mr. Kephart. Would you please come with us?" he requested.

"I would prefer not to," Robert replied.

The gun pressed harder into his back. "I'm sorry, Mr. Kephart. I guess I shouldn't have posed that as a question. You *will* come with us, *now*. Give my friend here the keys to your car, please."

Robert handed the man his keys. They put Robert in the backseat of his car, and the man with the gun slid in next to him. The other got behind the wheel and started the engine. Robert would never be seen again. He was loaded into a private Lear jet, and thrown out somewhere over the Pacific Ocean.

Chapter Thirteen

Geneva—1996

We touched down in Geneva fairly early in the morning. I exchanged some of my currency for francs, and secured a taxi to take me to a hotel. A young man, who was on my flight, asked if we could share the cab. We had spoken briefly several times during the long flight, and he seemed harmless enough. He introduced himself as Steve, an engineering student from UC Santa Barbara. He carried a backpack, searching for adventure while in Europe on his summer break from school. I agreed to share the ride, and we loaded his backpack into the trunk.

As the taxi made its way through the narrow, winding streets, I gazed out the window. I watched with pleasure as small shops and cafés readied themselves for the day's business. Tables were being set, and people were talking and laughing as they tended to their work. The taxi driver took me to the Rhône River Hotel, a beautiful building situated on the river that shared its name. I told Steve I insisted on covering the taxi fare. He thanked me for my generosity as he removed his backpack from the trunk, and disappeared into a crowd of people gathered on the sidewalk. I paid the taxi driver, then tried to calculate what the tip should be, in francs. I finally settled on what I thought was the correct amount, then watched his expression as I handed it to him. He seemed neither disappointed nor elated, so I assumed that either I calculated correctly, or he was one heck of a poker player.

I checked in, and found my way to the room. I opened the curtains. The view of the Alps and the river was breathtaking. The clear blue sky played host to a dozen or so puffy clouds, dancing carelessly above the horizon. Their reflections, almost perfect mirror images, moved along with them on the glassy river below. I gazed out the window for a few moments, watching the sailboats skim across the smooth water, and thought of my beautiful *Plan B,* now a pile of charred teak and melted fiberglass at the bottom of Uncle Doug's harbor. I choked back the tears that began to well up. Crying wouldn't help my situation.

I looked around the room. The furnishings were darker than I liked, but it was a nice-enough room. I bounced once or twice on the bed; it seemed comfortable. Most important, the bathroom was clean, and well stocked with towels. I splashed some water on my face, attempting to overcome the effects of jet lag. Wearing the same clothes I had put on the night my boat exploded, I looked and felt like a mess. I couldn't remember how long ago that was—it seemed like an eternity. I wasn't even sure what day of the week it was. What I did know for sure was that I needed to get some fresh clothes, and a toothbrush. I pulled the airline boarding pass from my jeans pocket to throw away. Some folded papers came out with it, and fell to the floor. I picked up the papers and unfolded them. They were the pages from Robert Kephart's address book. I had forgotten I put them in my pocket after I made the call to Kerstin. I assumed they were destroyed in the fire. Good. That would save me having to search for her. I put her address back in my pocket, along with the room key, and let myself out into the hallway.

I made my way down through the lobby, and out onto the street. I didn't have to go far to find shopping. I picked up enough clothing and undergarments to get me through several days. I bought a nice Italian purse, so I could get that wad of money out of my waistband. It was starting to feel very uncomfortable, and was irritating my skin. I also purchased some basic necessities—toothbrush, toothpaste, comb, etc. Then I sat at the cosmetic counter of an expensive department store, and let the girl working there give me a complete makeover. I laid a small fortune on the counter to pay for my purchase, and picked up my small bag of cosmetics.

Back in my hotel room, I put away my recent acquisitions, and lay down on the bed for a quick nap. My intention was to rest my eyes for fifteen minutes. Six hours later, I woke up hungry. I did a double take when I looked at the clock next to the bed. It was almost six o'clock. I changed my clothes, and walked down to the hotel restaurant. It seemed strange to order dinner—I felt more like having breakfast. I capped off my meal with a chocolate bar. I couldn't travel all the way to Switzerland and not get a taste of that famous sweet stuff.

I walked back through the lobby and out onto the street. I hailed a taxi, and showed him the address on my folded paper. Ten minutes later, we stopped in front of an older, neatly kept house. It was small, just like the rest of the homes on the block. There was a light on in what appeared to be the kitchen. I could see a woman through the window, either washing dishes or cooking—I couldn't tell which. I was about to leave the cab and go knock on her door, when a second figure appeared in the window. This one was a man. He came up from behind and put his arms around her, then kissed her on the neck. Finally, the taxi driver asked if this was the right address.

"Oh. I'm sorry. Yes. This is the right address," I said as I watched the couple in the window.

I thought to myself, *I should have called ahead of time.* This would not be a good time to meet with Kerstin. I would have to wait until tomorrow—after I'd had a chance to call to let her know that I was here. That way, we could meet in private. "Can you take me back to the hotel?" I asked.

His eyebrows rose and his bottom lip protruded as he pondered my request. "Certainly," he replied.

When I returned to the hotel, I placed a call to her. "Hello. Kerstin?"

"Yes. Who is this?" she asked.

"This is Devonie. Remember me?"

She hesitated. "Oh, yes. Devonie. How are you? Are you still safe?" she asked. The concern in her voice sounded sincere.

"Well, not exactly. I have a feeling I am going to need your help, after all. Can we meet tomorrow morning?"

"Of course. What's going on? Has something happened?"

"You could say that. Someone has killed a dear friend

of mine, and almost killed another. And the boat I live on was blown to smithereens.''

''Oh, my. Do you know who did it?'' she asked.

''The really scary thing is, I think the FBI may be behind it, at least the bombing of my boat, and the accident that nearly killed my friend. Does that sound likely to you?''

''It's very possible. I know that on several occasions, Robert worked closely with the CIA. There is another man; his name is Khan. He is the devil himself. You do not want to get anywhere near him, if you can help it.''

''Khan? How is he connected to Robert?'' I asked.

''He worked with Robert only once. The two of them had a falling-out of sorts, and Khan feels Robert still owes him. You need to make very certain Khan doesn't find you. He'll certainly harm you in order to get what he wants.''

''I'll do my best. I'll need you to help me identify these people that I'm supposed to be hiding from.''

''I will. Devonie, was there a computer in the things that you found of Robert's?''

I hesitated. The very person who told me to trust no one was now asking me to trust her. ''Yes, there was. . . . But there wasn't anything on it I found useful,'' I finally replied.

''Are you sure? Did you check everything?''

''I'm pretty sure, but I suppose I could have missed something. Why?''

''No reason. I'm sure that if you checked it, there probably isn't anything there. Where are you staying?'' she asked.

''I'm in Geneva. I'll meet you at the River Rhône Café. Do you know it?''

''Yes. Is nine too early?''

"That would be fine. I'll see you then. 'Bye," I said, and hung up the phone.

I booted up the laptop again. I had a feeling that Kerstin was more interested in that computer than she would have me believe. I checked all the directories again. There was nothing else that I hadn't already looked at. Frustrated, I shut the thing down and went to bed, but I couldn't fall asleep.

I had been dressed and ready to go since seven the next morning. Every five minutes, I impatiently checked the time on my watch. It would take only ten minutes to walk to the café to meet Kerstin. Finally, at eight-thirty, I left. I grabbed my purse, and let myself out of the room. I made my way down the long corridors and around the corners. I came up behind a couple who were strolling down the hallway, holding hands and speaking some romantic European language. It was one of those dialects that could make the phrase "Boy, that chili really repeated on me" sound as though he were offering her the moon on a silver platter.

The aisle was narrow. I forced myself to slow down and be patient. I kept my distance to give them and myself a comfort zone. There was no rush; I had plenty of time. When we all rounded the last corner into the hotel lobby, I spotted the two familiar faces, talking to the desk clerk. I stopped dead in my tracks and did an about-face. There was no way out to the street without walking right past them. I couldn't go back to my room—they were probably on their way there. I walked briskly down the hallway until I came upon a maid's cart, and let myself into the open room she was cleaning. The maid was busy in the bathroom, so I kept watch, peering out the small opening of the door, until I saw Cooper and Willis walk by. When they disappeared around the corner, I left the room, and hurried toward the front doors. Halfway across the lobby, the desk clerk spotted me, and hailed my name loudly enough that it could be heard all the way to the kitchen of the hotel restaurant.

"Miss Lace. You have some guests going up to visit you. I'm glad I caught you before you left, otherwise you would have missed them," he called out. *How did he even remember who I was?* I thought to myself, agitated. I must have made some sort of impression on him when I checked in.

"Thank you. I passed them on the way down," I answered, not slowing down as I made my way closer to the exit.

I turned to look over my shoulder just as Cooper rounded the corner and spotted me. Willis was right on his heels. I darted for the huge revolving glass doors, and pushed my way through.

"Wait! Stop, Miss Lace! We just want to talk to you," Cooper called out as I pushed my way out onto the sidewalk.

I started running, gaining about a half a block before they got out of the hotel lobby and chased after me. I was running and watching them behind me at the same time. I didn't notice the car ahead, with the open door. The man stepped out, and I ran right into him.

"Whoa, there," he said as he grabbed me to keep me from falling. Then he noticed the two men running after me. "Quick. Get in," he said as he shoved me into his car. I slid over to the passenger side. He jumped in, started the engine, and took off, just as Willis grabbed onto the door handle. He tried to hang on, but wasn't able to keep his grip as we accelerated out into the traffic.

I looked at him in amazement. "Craig. What in the world are you doing here?"

Chapter Fourteen

Craig didn't answer me immediately. He was too busy trying to drive in this unfamiliar territory, as he watched in his rearview mirror for my two pursuers. When it seemed we were safely out of the city limits and no one was following us, I initiated a conversation again.

"Okay. Now you can tell me what in the world you're doing here," I demanded.

"First things first," he said. "Are you okay?"

"I think so, but I don't know for how long. These guys are really persistent. I'm afraid that it's just a matter of time before my luck runs out."

"Well, if they can't find you, they can't catch you. I'm going to do my best to make sure they can't find you."

"Speaking of finding me, how did you know where I was?" I asked.

"It wasn't too difficult. I just followed you to your gate at the airport. After you boarded, I found a young college

127

student who was on your flight, and gave him a hundred dollars to follow you after you landed in Geneva. I told him there would be another hundred for him when he called me with the name of your hotel.''

''Ah, that would be Steve,'' I deduced.

''Yes. I believe Steve was his name. Nice kid.''

''Okay. Next question. Whatever possessed you to follow me here? Didn't I tell you that I didn't want you involved in this?''

''I can't help it. I have this uncontrollable need to rescue poor helpless creatures, who would otherwise be lost to the predators of this inhumane world,'' he said as he gave me a wink and a smile that could charm an angry grizzly into a teddy bear.

''I'm hardly a poor helpless creature,'' I stated emphatically, with a bit of ire in my voice. If there's one thing I am most proud of, that would be my independence.

''I know. I know,'' he replied in self-defense. ''I was just kidding. Please don't sentence me to the dungeon for my poor attempt at chivalry.''

''I'll grant you a pardon this time, but be aware that you're on probation; so you'd just better watch your step, mister,'' I teased. We both laughed, then the seriousness of my situation came hurtling back at me, and the smile left my face.

''Seriously. What possible reason could you have for being here? You hardly even know me, and you know nothing about my situation.''

''Well, that's not entirely true. After I ran into you at the airport, I canceled my trip to the medical conference, and went directly to your uncle. I told him about our encounter at the airport, and demanded to know what was going on. I told him I intended to follow you here, and the more I knew about your situation, the better I'd be able to help you. Arlene convinced him to tell me what he knew. I think she has a soft spot for me.''

"Oh, I'm sure of that," I interjected.

"Anyhow, he filled me in on the little bit of information he had. He also told me you hadn't really had a chance to give him all the details, since it seems you've been on the run from someone or another ever since you arrived in Del Mar. He did give me some information for you, and he wants you to call him just as soon as you can.''

"What sort of information?" I asked.

"Before you left, you gave him a diskette containing some E-mail documents?''

"Yes, that's right," I answered, anxiously awaiting the rest of the message.

"Well, he took it directly to his friend at the *Los Angeles Times*. The guy just about fell out of his chair when he read whatever was on that disk. Apparently, about a year ago, nearly every major newspaper in the country received a copy of an FAA report containing the page that was on your diskette. The anonymous informant appealed to anyone receiving the document to investigate the official record. He stated in a letter included with the report that the final version of the report contained nothing about the questionable device found in the wreckage, and that the device had disappeared from the collection of evidence found at the crash site.''

"You're kidding," I replied in amazement. "Did they investigate it?''

"I don't know about the other newspapers, but your uncle's friend did. He said he went directly to the FAA, and showed them the report he received. When questioned, the FAA officials insisted it was a hoax, initiated by some radical group trying to discredit the administration. The FAA actually produced hundreds of similar documents sent in by other, as they put it, 'extremists,' who supposedly unveiled the true cause of that crash. Some of them stated that aliens from another planet shot down the plane with lasers. Others claimed Russian satellites were responsible. One guy even accused his mother-in-law of putting a bomb on the plane, because he was supposed to be on the flight. Anyhow, the report was labeled as a hoax, and tossed in a pile with all the other discredited accounts of the accident.''

"So, now that this missing page has turned up again, are they reconsidering the validity of the informant's claims?" I postulated.

"Your uncle's friend says it sure looks a lot more promising than it did a year ago, but he won't do anything with it unless he meets with the anonymous informant to establish some sort of credibility."

"Great. Except that I haven't a clue who the informant is. It had to be someone involved in the investigation, or someone close to one of the investigators. Whoever it is must be afraid for his life, if he can't come forward with the evidence required to reopen the investigation. Somehow, I think our own government is involved. Why else would the FBI want me out of the picture?"

"FBI? What have they got to do with this?" Craig asked.

"Those two guys who were chasing me in Geneva were FBI agents. No one knew where I was staying in Del Mar, and no one knew about Jason's involvement in this whole thing, until I went to talk to them. That very night, my boat was destroyed, and Jason was almost killed. Oh, poor Jason. How is he? Were you able to get some protection for him?"

"You don't need to worry about Jason. The director over at the Med Center in Los Angeles is a good friend of mine. I had him transferred up there, and arranged for his records to be 'adjusted,' per my instructions. As of today, Jason's identity is that of a Mr. Juan Fernandez. Anyone looking for Jason Walters in any hospital in Southern California will be sadly disappointed."

"What about his family? Aren't they going to wonder what this is all about?" I asked.

"I met with his family, and explained that they were better equipped up in Los Angeles for taking care of Jason. They didn't seem to mind, especially since they live in Glendale, and the commute to the hospital is much shorter."

"That's good. How is he doing otherwise? Is he out of the coma yet?"

"I checked on him before they transported him. He was awake and asking for you. I explained to him that you were okay, and that he needed to stay under wraps until this whole thing blows over. He seemed to get the drift. Medically, he's going to be okay."

"That's somewhat of a relief, but I'm not sure how this is ever going to 'blow over,' as you put it."

"One thing's for sure. We need to get you in a safe hiding place. Then we should concentrate on finding out who this mysterious informant is, and what this FAA report is all about. If there's government involvement in some sort of conspiracy, your only hope is going to be to expose it big-time—blow the whole thing out of the water."

"Like they did to my boat?"

"Exactly."

"I know you're not going to like what I'm about to tell you. You have to take me back to the hotel," I told him.

"What? Why in the world would you want to go back there? Those two agents will be watching your room around the clock."

"I know, but I have to get the computer. I think there's something very important on it."

"What is it?"

"I don't know. I haven't found it yet, but I will," I answered.

"Well, you can't go back there. Tell me where it is, and I'll figure out a way to get it," he said.

After dark, we returned to Geneva and parked a short distance from the hotel.

"You stay here. I'll just slip in, grab the computer, and slip back out," Craig said with confidence.

"How do you intend to do that? Aren't you the one who said they'd be watching my room?"

"Don't worry. I'll find some supply closet, and disguise myself as a bellboy. They do it in the movies all the time."

"Now, why would a bellboy be going to an empty room?" I quizzed.

He thought for a moment. "Okay. I'll disguise myself as a maid. They're always going into empty rooms."

"Yeah, right. A six-foot-two maid with hairy arms and legs and a five-o'clock shadow. They'd never catch on to that," I quipped.

"Well, they might not. They *are* government workers, you know."

"Very funny. We need a plan. I have an idea. I'm going to try to lure them away from the hotel. Can you camp out in the lobby, and watch for them to leave?"

"Okay. What's your plan?"

"They must have someone monitoring all airline ticket purchases. How else would they have known to follow me here? I'll just go out to the airport, buy a ticket on the next flight back to the States, and they'll rush out there to try to catch me. After you see that they've left, you can use my key to sneak in, and grab the computer. I stuffed it behind the headboard of the bed.''

''Okay. Then you meet me right here as soon as you can.''

''Right. Oh . . . and Craig . . . while you're in there, could you grab the little teal blue sweater hanging in the closet? It cost me sixty bucks, and I haven't even worn it yet.''

''Yes, dear. Anything else?''

''No. That should do it. Here's the key. I'll see you back here as soon as I can. Good luck.''

I collected the newly purchased airline ticket, along with my passport, and stuffed them into my purse. I walked briskly away from the ticket counter, toward the long corridors leading to the exits. I left the car parked in the unloading zone, with the driver-side door open. I just needed to hurry back out of the terminal, and meet up with Craig.

I rounded a corner, and passed two men wearing blue suits and skinny black ties. I smirked, and thought how much they looked like the computer geeks I used to deal with back in college—when IBM had such a large market share in the industry. One talked on a cell phone, while the other flipped through a stack of photographs. Then I heard the one on the phone say, ''She just bought it?''

I stopped and turned. So did they. We stared one another down for a brief moment, then the one with the photos pointed an accusing finger at me. ''That's her!''

I broke into a full run, darting around and through the masses of people crowding the corridors. They were right on my tail. I ran track in high school—the hundred-yard dash was my event. My legs reminded me that eighteen years was a long time ago. Those two FBI agents behind me may have looked like geeks in their bland suits, but they ran as if they had just graduated from the academy. I rounded a corner, and spotted my only hope of losing these guys—a group of about seventy-five Japanese tourists. I quickly squeezed my way into the middle of the crowd, and waited for my pursuers to pass. When they realized they had lost me, they split up—each going down a separate corridor. I slipped back out of the crowd, and headed in the opposite direction.

I pushed my way through an emergency exit. The alarms began blaring. I couldn't tell which way the terminal parking was. I seemed to be on the runway side of the building. I jogged along the dimly lit wall, and rounded the corner. There, on the other side of an eight-foot chain-link fence topped with barbed wire, was the roadway to the short- and long-term parking areas. I needed only to climb over, and determine if I should go left or right, to get to the car.

I started to climb. I gingerly maneuvered one leg over the barbed wire. So far, so good. Then I tried swinging the other leg over, but my jeans leg caught a barb. I found myself performing the splits on top of the fence. I finally managed to make some slack in the fabric, and release my leg from the grip of the nasty barb. As soon as I freed my leg, I slipped, and fell eight feet to the concrete below.

I lay motionless for about a minute. I performed a mental examination of my body's state. Nothing felt broken. I dragged myself up to my feet. My legs seemed to be working. I glanced left, then right. I spotted the United Airlines terminal sign—where I parked the car. I hurried along the rows of cars, and pushed my way through crowds of people. A couple of airport security officials were standing next to my car, discussing the possibility of towing it.

"I'll move it. I'm sorry. Please don't tow it away. I got tied up," I assured them.

"Is this your car?" one of them asked.

"Yes. I'll get it right out of here."

"Make sure you do. This zone is for loading and unloading passengers only."

"I understand. It won't happen again," I reassured them, as I slid into the driver's seat and closed the door.

As I pulled away from the curb, I spotted my two pursuers, frantically searching the area. I eased into the flow of traffic, and slunk away—unnoticed.

I met up with Craig at our predetermined meeting place. He had successfully retrieved the computer, and my teal sweater, just as we planned. By the time Cooper and Willis realized I wasn't on the plane, Craig and I were on our way out of Geneva, and headed toward Paris.

Chapter Fifteen

We managed to find a private charter service at a small airfield outside of Paris that took us into Italy. I spread the word at the airport that I was interested in chartering a private jet to the United States, and that money was no object. Within thirty minutes, I had a string of Italian pilots offering their services. After interviewing a few of them, and inspecting their planes, I agreed to deal with the one who asked the fewest questions. I asked the pilot how soon he could be ready to take off.

"We can go anytime. Actually, our home base is in Florida. I just flew Arnold over yesterday for a short vacation. He's the president of the company that owns the plane. I'll fly back to the States today and return next week to pick him up. The plane is fueled, wet bar and galley are stocked, and we're ready to go."

"Great. I just need to make one phone call before we leave," I said, anxious to get in the air.

136

I phoned Kerstin, and explained I had to flee the country quickly, and I would be back in touch with her as soon as I could. She seemed distressed that we hadn't gotten a chance to meet.

Craig and I gathered the little gear we had, and boarded the jet. "What a beautiful plane," I said, admiring the exquisite aircraft. The plush carpeting and overstuffed captain's chairs gave more the feeling of entering someone's living room, rather than a flying bus—a nearly two-million-dollar flying bus.

"She *is* a beauty, isn't she?" Larry, the pilot, replied proudly. "She's a Lockheed VC-140B Jetstar. Her wingspan is nearly fifty-five feet. She's over sixty feet long, and almost twenty-one feet high. She weighs out at about forty-one thousand pounds, and is powered by four Pratt and Whitney J-60 turbojets, with three thousand pounds' thrust each."

"Wow. Sounds like we could give the *Enterprise* a run for her money. How fast can she fly?" I asked, anxious to know how soon we'd be back in the States.

"She'll max out at nearly six hundred miles per hour, but our cruising speed is about five hundred and twenty."

Another man boarded the jet and closed the cabin door behind him. "All set, Larry. Let's hit it," he said enthusiastically.

"Okay. Al, here, is our copilot," Larry said. "Al. This is Devonie and Craig. They needed a lift back to the States, and I told them we could accommodate them."

"Great," Al said. "You folks vacationing here?"

Larry cut in. "We're not supposed to ask them any questions, Al. Devonie, here, has purchased a first-class ticket with our little airline, and she has paid a premium for her privacy. I'll split the proceeds with you, but you have to agree to her terms,'' Larry said as he showed Al the bundle of cash I had given him.

''Great. Looks like I'll be able to put that pool in, after all,'' Al jested. ''You folks just take a seat right here, and fasten your seat belts. We'll be in the air soon. After we get to our cruising altitude, I'll put on my flight attendant hat, and dig something up from the galley. Hope you folks like prime rib.''

''Sounds wonderful,'' I said as I settled into one of the seats, and fastened myself in.

I hadn't had so much fun on a flight since I was eight years old, the first time I rode the rocket-ship ride at Disneyland. The prime rib was perfect, the salad superb, and Al proved to be very entertaining. He told us jokes, and recounted humorous stories all the way across the Atlantic. After we all treated ourselves to Coffee Almond Crunch Häagen-Dazs bars, Larry actually let me fly the plane. I banked turns to the left, then right. I learned about yaw and pitch and stalls. I think I made Craig a little nervous. I was almost disappointed when I had to relinquish the controls so we could touch down in Miami.

''Thank you both so much,'' I said to Larry and Al, as we stepped off the Jetstar. I looked back at the plane, and noticed her name painted on the side. *The Magic Carpet. How appropriate,* I thought.

''Listen, Craig. I'm going to stay here in Florida for a while. They shouldn't be able to find me here—at least for the time being. I think you should go on back to San Diego, and let Uncle Doug know I'm okay.'' I couldn't let him know my real motivation for wanting him to go on ahead without me. I was beginning to feel too comfortable with him. I found myself relying on him to share the burden of the load I was carrying, and I couldn't let that happen. Too dangerous. Better to face the murderous villains who were after me than to let anyone get close to my heart. If I had to, I'd be cold and rude so he would go. That had always worked in the past.

"No way. I'm not leaving you alone to fend for yourself, Devonie," he insisted.

"I'll be fine. I can take care of myself. Besides, so far, they don't know who you are. I sure would hate for them to go after you, like they did Jason."

"They won't come after me. And as far as letting your Uncle Doug know you're okay, you can call him yourself."

"No. I don't think I should chance it. I'm sure they're tapping his phone. They could probably trace any call right back to me. No. I really wish you'd do what I ask, Craig. I'll be fine here, as long as I keep a low profile. Besides, I'd like to get word to his contact at the *L.A. Times* about the FBI chasing me all the way to Europe. You could do that for me."

It took a lot of convincing, but I finally persuaded him. I saw him off on his flight back to San Diego, then caught a cab to a nearby hotel.

"I need to do some work from my room. Is there a modem phone connection available?" I requested at the front desk.

"Certainly, Miss Smith," the clerk replied. "All of our executive suites are well equipped for today's high-tech guests. You should find everything you need at the desk in your room. If you have any problems, just call down to the front desk, and we'll do our best to take care of you."

"Thank you," I said.

I fumbled with the laptop, trying to figure out which port was for the modem. I dug through a collection of adapters I found in the desk drawer, and finally got the correct configuration. I plugged the phone cord into the computer, and powered it up. Robert Kephart had apparently subscribed to an Internet service provider, and had installed the short-cut to the network connection on the computer's desktop. Chances were that his account had expired by now, but I tried the connection anyway. Kephart had checked the SAVE PASSWORD boxes, so I didn't have to guess what it might be. Surprisingly, I was logged right into the network. He must have prepaid his account, or else had his payments directly taken from an existing credit card account. It looked like my luck might be changing. I opened the In-ternet explorer, and started my search. I entered my search criteria—*Flight 9602*. There were about five hundred matches returned. I started at the top of the list, and began reading articles. Several hours had gone by, and I hadn't found anything that helped in any way. I ordered room service, and had dinner sent up. By three in the morning, I was ready to give up for the night and get some sleep. I decided to check the last entry in the group I was working on, before turning in. I clicked on the title, and waited for the page to build.

A very simple page painted itself in front of me. It con-tained only a button with a picture of an envelope on it. I clicked on the button, and was brought into an E-mail ed-itor. I began typing:

I have come across some evidence that would indicate the crash of Flight 9602 was not due to pilot error, as the official FAA report states. Possibly, some elec-tronic device may have been present on the plane that caused the navigation equipment to malfunction. There seems to be some danger in reporting this evi-dence to the officials, as I have found myself in fear for my life. If you can help me, I would greatly appreciate it.

I delivered the mail to the E-mail box, closed down the Internet explorer, disconnected the phone connection, and shut down the computer. I laid my head on the pillow, and shut my eyes. The two-headed snake continued to torment me from the sandy beach in my dream.

Chapter Sixteen

Amanda Powers was sitting slumped in the bathroom when the doorbell rang. She had been crying and fighting nausea all morning. The morning sickness hadn't subsided as the doctor had hoped, but she was reluctant to take any of the drugs offered to her. Her mother-in-law answered the door. It was the mailman delivering a package. Emily brought it into the bathroom for her mother.

"Look, Mommy. It's a present," she said innocently.

Amanda lifted her head, glancing at the box. It was a package from David. The funeral had been over two weeks ago. He had mailed it from Mexico, the day he left on that horrible flight. She reached over, and took the package from the little girl.

"Thank you, sweetie," she said as she laid the box on the floor next to her.

"Aren't you going to open it?" Emily questioned, anxious to see the contents of the mysterious package.

"Not now, honey. Mommy is too sick right now. Maybe later. Okay?"

"Okay, Mommy . . ." With affection ringing in her voice, Emily continued, "Grandma wants to know if you want some tea or soda crackers. She said it might make you feel better."

"Tell Grandma no thank you, honey. I think I'll just sit here for a little while."

"Okay, Mommy," Emily said as she left her mother sitting on the bathroom floor.

Amanda fingered the package sitting on the floor next to her. It was addressed to Queen Amanda and Princess Emily. She closed her eyes, laid her head on her folded arms, and began sobbing, again.

Later in the day, when the nausea had subsided, Amanda gathered up Emily and the package, and sat down on the sofa.

"Who's the present from?" Emily asked. Her big blue eyes sparkled with anticipation.

"It's from your daddy, sweetie. He mailed it a long time ago—before he went to Heaven."

"He did?"

It pained Amanda to see the confusion in Emily's face.

Amanda carefully opened the package. "Oh, look, honey," she said as she pulled out a pair of string puppets from Mexico. The señor played a guitar; the dancing señorita held castanets. "Daddy sent these for you."

Emily squealed with delight. "How do they work?" she asked.

Amanda handed the puppets to her mother-in-law, Martha. "Maybe Grandma can show you how to work them."

"Oh, sure I can, sweetheart. Here. You just take these little sticks, and make them do silly dances. See?"

Emily giggled uncontrollably at the puppets.

Amanda took a small box out of the larger package. She opened it slowly. The delicate, silver heart-shaped locket dangled from her shaking fingers. On the back, the inscription read: *David loves Amanda—Forever.* Again, Amanda fought back the tears welling up. She didn't want to cry in front of Emily anymore. The little girl needed her mother to be strong for her right now.

Amanda retrieved another smaller package from the box. It contained a computer CD, and a note from David. The note read:

Dear Amanda,

Just wanted to send a small token of my love for my girls. I miss you both so much. I can't wait to get home. I know how slow the mail takes to get from Mexico to the States, so I will have been home for weeks by the time you open this. But I will probably be at work when it arrives, so just put this CD in my desk, and I'll take care of it tonight, when I get home.

Love,

David

"What did Daddy send you, Mommy?" Emily asked.

"He sent me this beautiful locket. See?" Amanda said as she dangled the silver heart in front of the little girl's big blue eyes.

"Oh, how pretty," Emily exclaimed.

Martha noticed the CD, and the note Amanda held in her shaking hands. "What's in the envelope?" she asked.

"I don't know. David's letter says to just put it in his desk. For now, that's what I'm going to do."

"Here. Let me put it away for you, Amanda," Martha said as she took the envelope and walked into the study. "I'll just put it in the top drawer," she called to her daughter-in-law as she laid the envelope in the drawer, and closed it.

"Thanks, Martha," Amanda said. "I really appreciate all the time you're spending here with us, but I know you need to get back to Neil. Don't feel like you have to stay and take care of me. Poor Neil needs you so much right now. Is he feeling any better, now that the chemotherapy is done?"

"Oh, he's feeling a little better. Don't you worry about Neil or me right now, Amanda. I can spend the mornings here with you, until your morning sickness passes," Martha assured her.

"Okay, Martha, but I'm feeling fine now. Don't feel like you need to stay, if you want to get home."

"Okay. I get the hint. I know when I'm not wanted," Martha joshed.

"Now, you know you're always wanted around here."

"I know, honey. I'm just teasing. I think I will head back home now—if you're really feeling better."

"I am, Martha. Thank you so much."

" 'Bye, then. Come here and give me a big hug and kiss, Miss Emily," she said to her granddaughter.

" 'Bye, Grandma," Emily said as she wrapped her arms around her grandmother.

"Good-bye, Amanda. I'll be over in the morning, to see how you're doing."

"Okay, Martha. Thanks, again . . . so much," Amanda said as they walked to the door.

Amanda put Emily down for a nap, then lay down on the queen-size bed she had grown accustomed to sharing with David, and wept.

Chapter Seventeen

Florida—1996

It was past ten o'clock when I woke up. I made my way
to the bathroom and took a nice long shower, to try to wake
myself up. I missed the hotel's complimentary continental
breakfast, so I went to the hotel restaurant and ordered fresh
fruit and a bowl of cereal. When I returned to my room, I
logged back onto the Internet, to continue my search. I was
notified I had E-mail. I opened the in-box, and read the
message. It simply read: *Press this button to notify and
meet me in my chat room.* I followed the instructions, and
waited. Several minutes passed, then some text came across
the screen.

"Who are you?" it read.

I entered, *"Who are you?"*

"I asked first," came the reply.

"My name is Devonie. I'm nobody, really. Just an in-

nocent bystander who got caught up in a real nightmare," I typed.

"Do you have any connection with the CIA, FBI, DEA, or FAA?" the mysterious correspondent asked.

"No. I'm just a self-employed treasure hunter, who stumbled upon a very dangerous prize. What's your connection with Flight 9602?"

"I know the real cause of the crash. I was at the crash site. I uncovered evidence that would substantiate your theory about the electronic device," was the reply.

I read the words on the screen, but they somehow seemed unreal. The open windows in my hotel room kept a steady flow of hot, humid air blowing on my perspiring skin. Even with the heat, a chill ran up my spine.

Again, I typed, *"Who are you?"*

"That isn't important. Like yourself, my safety has been jeopardized, and I need to stay anonymous—for my own health. Do you still have the device you found?"

"No. The FBI took it," I answered.

"I thought you said you had no connection with the FBI."

"I thought you meant, did I work for them. I found the device, along with some other incriminating evidence, and reported it to the FBI. Shortly after, the boat I live on was destroyed in an explosion, and I've been on the run ever since."

"I see. Explosions seem to be the method of choice for solving their problems," came the reply.

"Who are 'they'?" I asked.

"I'm pretty sure it's the CIA. Of course, they would be acting in the interest of some higher authority. My guess is, it goes all the way to the White House. Are you familiar with the names David Powers and Michael Norris?"

"Yes. They were two DEA agents killed in the plane crash. How do they fit into this whole mess?"

"Over the past year, I've done some investigating of my own. Powers and Norris were working to shut down a major drug cartel in Mexico. My guess is, they were stepping on some pretty big toes."

"And whoever belonged to those toes, must have pretty big feet, too. Big enough to step on Powers and Norris, like a couple of ants on the sidewalk," I responded.

"Exactly. The problem is, unless someone comes up with some hard evidence, and gets it into the right hands, people like you and me are condemned to a life of running and hiding."

"What kind of evidence would it take?" I asked.

"That device you found would have been a good start, although it wouldn't prove anything. The actual device that brought the plane down is long gone, I'm sure. For a short while, I was corresponding with someone inside the FAA organization, who was suspicious about the disappearance of the original box. When he quit answering my E-mail, I decided to check up on him. I discovered that he had been killed."

"Was his name Frank Eastwood?" I asked, remembering the name of the FAA inspector who originally reported finding the device.

"No," was the reply.

"I have copies of E-mail documents that prove a contract existed to assassinate the two agents. I'm not sure how they would stand up as evidence in something like this."

"By themselves, they probably wouldn't carry much weight, but if we can come up with something more, they may prove to be very valuable."

"How much do you know about the two agents who were killed? Maybe they left some evidence behind that could be useful," I typed.

"Any evidence they had was destroyed with them in the crash. If there was any other evidence, it has all mysteriously disappeared. I have used all my available resources to check on the Mexican cartel drug investigation, and have come up with a big fat zero. As far as the DEA is concerned, there was never any operation in existence to shut down the cartel."

"That's crazy. There has to be someone out there who knew what they were working on."

"Oh, sure there is, but have you come up with a foolproof way to identify who you can trust? And what about getting someone killed because they tried to help. Can you live with that?"

"No. I guess you're right. But I have an idea. Can I reach you anytime using this connection?"

"Pretty much anytime. Why? What are you up to?"

"It's a long shot. I'll fill you in if it turns up anything," I replied.

"Okay. Good luck."

"Thanks. I'll need it. 'Bye," I typed, then exited from the chat room.

Before I closed down the Internet connection, I reread one of the articles about the crash of Flight 9602. David Powers was survived by his wife and daughter, who lived in San Diego. I used all the people search engines I could find to see if I could turn up an address on Amanda Powers, but nothing came up. I would have been surprised to find a DEA agent's family listed in the phone book. I dialed information, and requested the number of someone I knew could help—if only he would.

"Hello. Spencer?" I asked.

"Yeah. Who's this?" he asked, in a tone conveying a sense of caution. He sounded as if he thought he were talking to a ghost.

"Spencer. It's me, Devonie."

There was a long pause. "Spencer? Are you there? It really is me, Devonie," I repeated.

"I thought it sounded like you, but you're supposed to be dead. What the heck's going on, Dev? I went and made a fool of myself at your funeral and everything. I think I even cried, or something stupid like that. And now, you're not even really dead? What a friend you turned out to be."

"Take it easy, Spencer. I can explain everything. Just settle down," I reassured him. "Did you really cry?" I asked, a little amused, and touched that he would admit to such an untypical display of emotion.

"Darn right, I cried. Crocodile tears and runny nose. The whole nine yards. If you weren't a woman, I'd scratch 'Lying Dog' into the side of your car. You better have a darn good explanation, Miss Devonie Lace, or I swear, I'll put your name on every telemarketing call list in the country. You'll never be able to eat dinner in peace again."

"Oh, please. No. Not the telemarketing torture. Anything but that. Please have mercy on me, Spencer," I begged playfully.

"Okay. Start talking, sister. But remember, I've got my finger on the big TM button."

"Okay, Spencer. Here it is, in a nutshell: I've discovered some evidence implicating the CIA, FBI, DEA, FAA, and any other acronym you can think of, in the assassination of two DEA agents last year. I reported it to the FBI, and you saw what they did to my boat. I had to let everyone think I was dead, to save myself. Right now, I need your help, to get the address of Amanda Powers. She's the wife of one of the DEA agents who was killed. You should know, if anyone discovers you're helping me, you could be in a lot of danger. So, will you do it?'' I pleaded.

Spencer made a nasal ''wrong answer'' buzzer sound into the phone, and said, ''Sorry, Dev. One more chance, then I'm putting your name in the big telemarketing database in the sky, never to be deleted.''

''I swear it's true, Spencer. I'm not pulling your leg. I won't blame you if you don't want to help me. It's really dangerous, but you're the only person I know who can get into the records of people who don't want to be found.''

Spencer hesitated. ''Holy cow. You're serious. Aren't you?''

''I'm dead serious, Spencer. Do you think you can do it without anyone finding out?''

''You kidding? This is Spencer—the king of database hackers. A piece of cake.''

''Are you sure? I don't want you to get caught, or killed, or anything,'' I said, worried about his probation.

''Oh, heck. No need to worry about me. I can be in and out, and no one will ever know I was there. I'll have it for you in a couple hours. Where can I call you?'' he asked.

''You can E-mail it to me at this address: rkephart@seaside.com. Please be careful, Spencer.''

''I will, Dev. You just watch yourself. Hear me?''

''I will. Oh . . . and Spencer . . . did I ever tell you how much I admire your colorful use of the English language?''

''Every day of my life, when we worked together. Don't you remember? I never saw a person blush as much as you did. It got to be a regular challenge, to see what shade of red I could turn your face.''

"I'm glad I was a source of entertainment for you. Thanks for your help, Spencer."

"No problem. 'Bye, Dev," he said, then hung up the phone.

I turned my attention back to the computer sitting on the desk in front of me. I unconsciously danced the mouse pointer around the screen, while I thought about what I should do next. That VideoService icon just kept glaring at me. What was it? I had time to kill, so I clicked on the icon, and launched the application. I wasn't quite prepared for what I stumbled upon. VideoService didn't have anything at all to do with movies, as I had earlier suspected. This was a Swiss on-line service—designed to manage bank accounts. Once again, Mr. Kephart had saved his password, so I proceeded to connect to the bank account, and browse the available screens. It didn't take long to figure out how to navigate around the many options. I found a menu option for balance information, and clicked it. A bright blue screen painted before my eyes, and figures began scrolling down the page. At the bottom, a final to-tal—with yesterday's date. I blinked and rubbed my eyes to make sure I was reading it clearly. Could that figure actually be thirty-eight million dollars?

Chapter Eighteen

I checked the E-mail box two hours later. Nothing. I checked again, every hour on the hour. I began to worry that Spencer was having trouble. It was late. I picked up the phone, and dialed his number. No answer. Now I was really worried. Had I gotten Spencer into the same trouble I'd inflicted on Jason and Joe? Finally, at almost midnight, the message came through. Along with Amanda Powers's address, he wrote a short note:

Sorry it took so long to get this to you. Someone has really gone to a lot of trouble to make sure no one looks up your friend Amanda. I decided to use a client machine at the office, to ensure nothing could be traced to my house. You be careful, Devonie. I don't want to go through another one of your funerals— again.

Spencer had come through for me. I checked out of the hotel early the next morning, and caught the next flight to San Diego. The taxi dropped me at the address Spencer relayed. It was a cute little New England–style house, located right on the water. I rang the bell, and waited. A little girl, in blond pigtails, opened the door.

"Hi. Is your mommy home?" I asked.

From another room, I heard the voice of a woman. "Who is it, Emily?"

"I don't know, Mommy. It's a lady," the little girl called back.

Immediately, a woman came to the door to see who it was. She had a baby on one hip, and a bottle in her other hand.

"Hello. Can I help you?" she asked.

"Are you Amanda Powers?"

"Yes. I am," she answered, with a little hesitation.

"Hello, Mrs. Powers. My name is Devonie Lace. I wonder if I can talk to you about your late husband?"

"David?"

"Yes. It's very important. I won't take up too much of your time."

"Well, I'm not sure. . . ." Amanda shifted the baby to her other hip, and checked her watch.

"Please, Amanda. It could be a matter of life or death," I pleaded.

She reconsidered. "You said your name is Devonie?"

"Yes. Devonie Lace."

"Come in, Devonie. Just let me see if I can get my mother-in-law to take the baby for a while so we can talk," she said as she opened the door wider to let me in.

"Honey, go see if Grandma can come in from the garden

to help me with Eric for a little while. Okay?'' she asked the little girl.

''Okay, Mommy,'' she replied, and skipped off toward the backyard.

''Please. Sit down,'' Amanda said as she gestured me toward a sofa in the living room.

An older woman entered the room. ''Emily said you need help with Eric?''

''Oh. Hi, Mom. Devonie, this is my mother-in-law, Martha. This is Devonie Lace, Mom. I wonder if you can take Eric and put him down for his nap, so I can talk with her?''

''Certainly. It's nice to meet you, Devonie,'' the woman responded, as she took the baby from Amanda and carried him into another room.

''Now. What is it you want to talk about?'' Amanda asked.

''Amanda, did you know anything about what your husband was working on when he died?''

''Well . . .'' She thought for a moment. ''As I recall, he was working on a case with the Mexican government. They were investigating one of the many drug suppliers down there.''

''Did he tell you anything about what he found while he was there?'' I asked.

''No. He never talked much about his work. Everything was always very hush-hush, you know. Why do you want to know?''

''Amanda, I think the plane crash that killed your husband and his partner, along with all those other people, was no accident.''

She stared at me. ''What? No accident? What do you mean?''

''I think your husband and his partner stumbled onto

something very sensitive, and they were killed to shut them up.''

''Killed by whom? The Mexican drug producers?''

''No. I know they would seem like the logical suspects, but I'm afraid that someone else caused that plane to crash,'' I answered.

''Who?''

''Amanda, I think it's possible that someone within our own government was responsible for destroying that plane, to keep your husband and his partner quiet.''

A look of skepticism spread across her face. ''That's preposterous. Where would you ever get an idea like that?''

''I know it sounds incredible, but it's true. Are you sure your husband never mentioned anything? Or maybe he kept some records, or notes about things he was working on?''

Amanda nervously twirled the silver locket she wore around her neck with her quivering fingers. I'm sure that, living with a DEA agent, she would have been warned about giving information to strangers. Her mother-in-law returned from putting the baby down, and took a seat in the chair next to the sofa.

''Well, what are you girls finding to talk about?'' she innocently asked.

''Devonie thinks someone in our government purposely caused the plane crash that killed David,'' Amanda said as she reached for the phone. ''I think I should call Victor, and see what he knows about this.''

''No. Please, Amanda. Hear me out, before you make that call,'' I pleaded.

The cheery smile left Martha's face. The deep lines that had developed on her forehead from months of worrying over her late husband—and her late son's family—grew deeper. She placed her own hand gently over Amanda's, and pushed the phone back into its cradle. ''Wait a minute, Amanda. Why don't you let her finish, before you call Victor. It couldn't hurt to hear her out. Could it?''

Amanda removed her hand from the phone, and started fingering the locket again. ''Well, I suppose it couldn't hurt to hear what she has to say.''

''Thank you, Amanda,'' I said as I unpacked the laptop from its case, and booted the little machine up.

I explained to the two women how I came to acquire the machine, and briefly described the events of the past few days. Then I opened the first E-mail document—the one that contained the pictures of David Powers and Michael Norris, and the direction to Robert Kephart to eliminate them. Amanda read the document silently, then placed a hand over her mouth. She bit her lip to squelch her emotions.

''There's more,'' I said as I proceeded to open the second document.

''No. I don't want to see any more. I know that David didn't keep any notes or files from his work—not here at home, anyway. I'm not sure how I can help you, Devonie.''

Martha finished reading the second document. She studied the little laptop computer, and noticed the small CD-ROM unit in the open case. ''Wait a minute, Amanda. Remember the CD he mailed here before he left Mexico?''

Amanda gave her a blank stare. ''I don't remember. That was such a horrible time. Wait . . . I sort of remember something like that, but I don't recall what I did with it.''

''You didn't do anything with it. I put it away in David's desk for you. Have you moved any of his things?''

''No. Everything is still where he left it in his office.''

Martha hurriedly left, and returned shortly with an envelope with a CD in it. ''Here. See what this has on it,'' she said as she handed me the envelope. I replaced the disk drive with the CD drive, and inserted the CD. Along with dozens of Word documents, I found one Read Me file in the directory, and opened it. It was a message to Victor from David:

> Victor: Pay dirt. Here are the documents I told you about. We were able to get copies of all of them. Some pretty big players are going to go down, after this stuff hits the fan. Who would ever think one of the biggest problems in America was being financed by the biggest banks in the U.S.? What do you think this is going to do to our cconomy? I predict another bailout. What do think?

Then I opened document after document. I could hardly believe my eyes. Billions of dollars in loans to a company whose major product lines included cocaine, heroin, marijuana, and methamphetamine.

"Wow. This is the evidence we need to blow this thing out of the water. Amanda, please let me take this and give it to someone who can do something with it."

"Okay. But what if someone asks about it?"

"*Do not* tell anyone about this. Especially, don't tell anyone I spoke with you. For your own safety, just forget I was ever here, and that this CD ever existed."

I packed up the equipment, and started for the door. Then I realized I didn't have any transportation. "Thank you so much, Amanda. You have no idea how much this information will help. Can I use your phone to call a taxi?" I asked. I glanced out the backyard window, and noticed one of the neighbors on his dock, polishing the chrome on his speedboat.

"Sure, you can use the phone. It's right there, on the table," she answered.

"Maybe I won't need to call after all. Is that your neighbor out there, working on his boat?" I asked, pointing in the direction of the dock.

Amanda peered out the window to see what had caught my attention. "Oh, yes. That's Aaron."

"I'll be right back, if I need to use the phone," I said as I walked out the door, and headed down to the dock.

"Hello, there," I said. He flashed a surprising smile at me that sent tingles up from my toes to my fingertips. Locks of sandy blond hair frolicked dangerously close to his piercing blue eyes, until he shook them out of the way. The muscles in his bare, tanned arms flexed as he put the final touches on a beautifully detailed speedboat.

The sleek machine looked as though it were traveling seventy miles per hour, just sitting there next to the dock.

"Are you Aaron?"

"That would be me. And you are?"

"I'm Devonie. That's a pretty fancy boat you've got there, Aaron. Looks like she's pretty fast."

"Fast isn't the word for it, Devonie," he boasted, as he continued to polish the chrome.

"You don't suppose I could hire you to run me up to the Lace Marina, in Del Mar?" I asked.

"Well . . ." He scratched his head, and thought for a moment. "It'll cost you, Devonie. Are you sure you can afford it?"

I pulled a hundred-dollar bill from my pocket, and handed it to him. "Will this be enough?" I asked.

Aaron looked at the bill, and smiled affirmatively. "Actually, I was thinking more along the lines of a six-pack, but this will do just fine. Any friend of Ben Franklin's a friend of mine. Hop in, and hang on.''

If that boat could have sprouted wings, I believe it would have flown. Actually, I think we *were* flying, half the time. What a rush it was, to feel the power of that engine lift us right out of the water. Quite a different sensation from the relaxing feeling of the *Plan B*. The warm sun on my face and the cool spray of water felt good. For a short time, I forgot about the trouble I was in, and enjoyed the moment.

Aaron dropped me on the dock of my uncle's marina. I thanked him for the lift.

''Anytime, Devonie—and hey, the next one's on the house,'' Aaron said as he helped me off the boat.

Chapter Nineteen

Uncle Doug was talking on the phone with a dealer on the East Coast when I walked into his office. He motioned for me to take a seat while he finished up his call.

"Yeah, Marv. That sounds great. You get a crew together to sail her over here, and I'll have her sold before she gets through the Panama Canal. Just fax me all the specs, and we'll be in touch. I've got to go. I'll call you next week. 'Bye," he said, and hung up the phone.

Then he turned his attention to me. "Devonie Lace. Where the heck have you been? Why haven't you called? We've been worried sick."

"I'm sorry, Uncle Doug. It was too dangerous to contact you. I'm sure the Feds and the CIA are tapping your phones by now. Can we go outside?" I suggested.

"Sure. Let's take a walk. I want to show you the new yacht I just got in yesterday."

"Okay," I said. We walked down the dock, toward a

162

beautiful vessel, tied up at the end of the landing. This had to be one of the most exquisite sailing crafts I'd ever laid my eyes on. She was an absolute work of art. Her lines were as appealing to the eye as a painting by any of the great masters. Every detail, down to the hatch handle, showed evidence of impeccable care. At one time, this boat was someone's pride and joy. I wondered why she was on the market.

"Wow. What a beauty," I said as I admired the luxury sailing yacht, appropriately named *The Jewel*. "Why would someone want to sell such a lovely boat?"

"The man who had her built passed away recently. He owned a small winery up in the Napa Valley. His widow didn't share her husband's love for sailing. The business he left her was struggling, so she decided to sell."

"Have you got a buyer for her?"

"Not yet. She sure is nice, isn't she? Won't be hard to find a buyer for this little jewel. Sixty feet of pure joy. That's what she is. She's got four double cabins, each with their own private heads. Fully equipped galley, every piece of navigation equipment you can imagine. Even has an autopilot. Take a look at this deck. Isn't that teak gorgeous?"

I ran my hand along the railing, remembering the feeling I had the first time I saw the *Plan B*. "She's exquisite," I said as I daydreamed about sailing somewhere in the clear blue waters of the Caribbean.

Then I remembered why I had come here, and was hurled out of my sweet daydream into the cold reality of my situation. "Uncle Doug, can we go meet your friend at the *Los Angeles Times*? I've got some new information that's really incredible. I think we can blow this thing right out of the water, pardon the expression."

"Sure. Right now?"

"If we could. It's really urgent."

"Let's go. I'll get George to watch the office for me. I'll meet you in the parking lot. I'm in the Ferrari today."

Peter Cunningham listened intently, and took notes as I described the events of the past few days to him. Then, with amazement, he read the documents I brought on the CD. He looked like a gold miner who'd just struck the mother lode.

"This is remarkable, Devonie. Where did you get it?"

"Is it important for you to know? I mean, I don't want to put any more people in danger."

"Well, it would help if I had some sort of witness. Of course, the identity of that person would be kept completely confidential."

I thought for a moment. "Can I use your phone connection for this laptop, Mr. Cunningham?"

He looked a little confused. "Sure. I guess so. What for?" he asked.

"I think I might have a witness for you—if we can convince him."

I made the connection, and signaled for a response from my newest chat-room acquaintance.

He came on-line, and requested my identity.

"Hello. It's Devonie," I typed.

"Hello, Devonie. What's happening?" he asked.

"I found the evidence we need. I'm sitting in the office of the Los Angeles Times'*s top investigative reporter. He's convinced that this new evidence—along with the copies of E-mail I had sent him earlier—can launch a full-blown Senate investigation. Indictments will surely be handed down, provided you agree to be a witness in the case."*

"I don't know. What kind of evidence did you get?"

"I found documents that implicate major U.S. banks and investors in the Mexican drug trade. Powers and Norris had copies of the documents with them when their plane crashed, but Powers made a backup, and mailed it to his wife, before he left Mexico. I have that backup, and have given it to Peter Cunningham, with the L.A. Times. *He would really like to meet with you. What do you think?"*

There was a long pause. Finally, a response came across the screen. *"I don't know. What kind of assurance do I have that my identity will be kept concealed? You and I both know the Witness Protection Program will be out of the question. That would be like assigning a hungry cat to protect a plump little mouse."*

Peter asked if he could respond. I slid the computer in front of him. *"This is Peter Cunningham, responding to your concerns,"* he typed. *"You have my personal guarantee that your identity will be held in the strictest confidence. If you know anything about me at all, then you know I have gone to jail on several occasions, for refusing to reveal my sources. I have people here who can be trusted to help protect you, until this thing goes to trial. I'm sure you're aware that I cannot absolutely one hundred percent guarantee your safety. But, I can promise you, I will never reveal you as a source, unless you otherwise advise me."*

Again, there was a pause. Finally, a response appeared on the screen. *"I'll have to think about this. I'll contact Mr. Cunningham within twenty-four hours with my answer."*

"Good enough. Thank you," Peter entered.

I took the little computer back, and closed down the connection. "Before I give you this CD, I want to copy it to my hard drive. It shouldn't take too long," I said to Peter.

''That's fine,'' he said as he continued making notes in his small tablet.

Uncle Doug was watching the file copy procedure with much interest. ''One of these days, I'm going to have to get myself up to speed on these darn computers,'' he said.

Peter laughed. ''I know what you mean, Doug. These young hotshot reporters—running around with their little notebook computers, downloading their stories right from the scene—are going to put me out of a job one of these days. I'm still getting by with this crazy little notepad, taking shorthand!''

I closed down the laptop, and put it back in its case. ''You're wrong about that. All the computers in the world will never replace the talent and skill people like the two of you have.''

''Thank you, Devonie,'' Peter replied. ''Let's keep in touch on this. I'm sure I'll have more questions for you, once I have gone through my notes. Hopefully, our mystery witness will come through for us, and we can bring a whole lot of people to justice. I realize I won't be able to contact you at my convenience, but if you can possibly check in with me daily?''

''Okay, Mr. Cunningham. Thank you,'' I replied.

Back at the Ferrari, Uncle Doug pulled a small key from his pocket. ''Here. Harv, down at the bank, had a replacement key for your safe-deposit box made for you.''

''Great. Thank you,'' I said as I took the key from him. ''Uncle Doug, do you still have that vacation house up at Tahoe?''

''The Incline Village house? Sure. Arlene and I go there at least four times a year. Say, that wouldn't be a bad place for you to hide out for a while.''

''That's exactly what I was thinking.''

"Let's stop back at the house and pick up the key. We can get you some transportation while we're at it."

"While we're there, I'm going to set you up with an E-mail address, so we can communicate without anyone listening in."

This time, transportation turned out to be Aunt Arlene's more conservative Camry. I stopped at a branch of my bank, and made a deposit of five thousand dollars into my checking account. Then I drove all night, and rolled into Tahoe at nearly three in the morning.

Chapter Twenty

I followed the directions on the map Uncle Doug had drawn for me. I found the house without too much trouble. I was here once, as a teenager, for a family Christmas vacation. Doug and Arlene invited the whole family for a week of fun in the snow. We skied and sledded and rode for miles on snowmobiles. We had a contest to see who could build the world's ugliest snowman—a competition that I won, hands down. We had snowball fights in the afternoons, and at night we roasted marshmallows in the fireplace. It was a really good time. I miss Christmases like that—when the whole family got together, and didn't worry about anything except whose turn it was to split wood for the fire.

I let myself into the house and turned on some lights. Uncle Doug called ahead, and had the kitchen stocked with food and supplies for me. I made myself a sandwich, and sat down at the big desk in the den. I was dead tired, but

I had one more job to do before retiring for the night. The time difference in Switzerland dictated that I take care of this business now. I hooked the phone line to the laptop and booted the little machine up. I connected one more time to VideoService, and noted the phone number of the Swiss Bank Corporation—the institution that housed Robert Kephart's account. I dialed the number, then waited for an answer.

"Hello. I'd like to find out about opening an account with your bank," I requested.

Surprisingly, it wasn't too difficult to open the account. I had to make a minimum deposit, which I made using an electronic funds transfer from my account, here in the States. I provided all the necessary information over the phone, and was faxed a form to fill out, sign, and fax back. I was informed I could begin making deposits immediately, but of course, there would be a seven- to ten-day period to complete the assignment.

Then, I connected again to the VideoService program and logged into Kephart's account. When I tried to generate a payment order, a dialogue box appeared in the center of the screen: *Please enter secondary confirmation password.*

I stared blankly at the screen. *Secondary password?* I wasn't prompted for this when I inquired on the account earlier. This additional security must be in effect for any transactions other than inquiries. I tapped my teeth with my fingernails, and ran the options through my head.

I dialed the bank's number again. "Hello. Can you please connect me with your information services manager?" I requested.

"One moment, please."

"Hello. Conrad Kobl speaking," a voice with a thick accent responded.

"Hello, Mr. Kobl. I wonder if you have a few minutes to participate in a brief information technology survey my company is conducting. I promise I will only require five minutes of your time."

"Oh, I don't know. I'm very busy. Can you call back later?" he replied.

"Mr. Kobl, I absolutely guarantee you'll be no more than five minutes with me. The responses to our questions will be published in *ComputerWorld* magazine. We may even want to visit your site, and shoot some photos for the issue. I have been given the authority to send you a wonderful free gift, if you agree to participate. What do you say?"

"Free gift?" he questioned.

"Yes, Mr. Kobl. If you agree to answer my questions, I'll send you a discount coupon, good for fifty dollars off any Microsoft software product you choose."

"Well, okay. Go ahead."

"Thank you, Mr. Kobl. First of all, what hardware platform are you currently on?"

"We're running on NCR servers now."

"NCR . . . I see. And what operating system?"

"UNIX. We are experimenting with a WindowsNT network, but it's for in-house use only, at this time."

"Very good. Tell me, Mr. Kobl, what is your application software platform?"

"We operate under a very popular banking package, provided by an outside vendor. We do have two in-house software developers who write specialized applications specific to our business."

"Do you use a relational database?"

"Yes. We use Oracle."

"I see. Thank you very much, Mr. Kobl. That's all the

questions I have for you. Watch for that discount coupon in the mail. Good-bye.''

I pressed the hook on the phone, then redialed the bank. "Hello. Please connect me to your human resources department."

"One moment, please."

"Hello. This is Caroline. How may I help you?"

"Hi, Caroline. My name is Trisha Yerington. I'm from Microsoft Corporation. I'm calling to confirm the attendance of two of your employees at our upcoming software developers' expo next month. Let's see, I have their names listed here, somewhere. What did I do with that list?" I fumbled with some papers on the desk.

"That would have to be Raul and Marie. They're our only programmers," she offered.

"Yes. I believe those are the names I have noted here. Gee. I can't seem to make out the last names. Could you confirm the spelling for me?"

"Sure. That's Raul Napoli and Marie Marcos. I'm checking our records, but I don't see anything about them being off-site for any conferences next month. Marie isn't here today, but I can check with Raul to see if it has just fallen through the cracks. Are you sure about this?"

"You know, you're right. It looks like they only requested information about the conference. I'll be sure to get that in the mail to them right away. Thank you for your help, Caroline."

"You're welcome. Good-bye."

"Good-bye."

I called the bank back. "Hello. May I speak with Raul Napoli, please?"

"One moment, please."

"This is Raul," the voice announced.

"Hello, Raul. This is Connie, from Oracle Worldwide Support. I've been assigned to troubleshoot a problem with your payroll system. Let's see, I have TAR number 455399-Od. Are you aware of the problem?"

"No. I didn't report any problems," Raul responded.

"No. It looks like a Marie Marcos reported the problem. She elevated the incident to the highest priority. Apparently, your payroll may not go through if we don't get this solved."

"I wasn't aware of any problem. Have you resolved it yet?" he asked.

"Well, not exactly. I haven't been able to log onto your UNIX box. The representative who wrote the trouble ticket must have botched the ROOT password. I've tried several times, but it keeps denying me. Can you please confirm the modem phone number and password for me?"

"Sure. Hang on a minute. I'll get that for you."

I carefully wrote down the information Raul so willingly supplied me. I remembered from past experience, whenever payroll is in jeopardy, normal security protocol gets tossed to the wind.

"Thanks, Raul. You should see me dialing in shortly. Hopefully, I'll have it solved in a jiffy. From what Marie reported, it sounds as though we just need to add a data file to your User-Data table-space."

"Just so we all get paid tomorrow. Let me know if you need anything else."

"I will. Good-bye."

I logged into the server, and assigned Robert Kephart a new password. This was almost too easy. Spencer would have been proud of me.

I connected to Kephart's account in VideoService again. This time, I sailed right through the secondary password—

"planb123." I issued a payment order to transfer funds to my new account, and assigned it an execution date of to-morrow. Then, I shut down the computer, found my way to a comfortable bed, and crashed.

Chapter Twenty-one

The next few days proved to be completely relaxing and uneventful. I communicated with Uncle Doug daily about the progress Peter Cunningham was making with the story. He told me our chat-room witness had shown up, but that was all he knew. Peter was not about to let out any information that could jeopardize the safety of the informant.

I sat down on the sofa with a dish of ice cream, and turned on the ten-o'clock news. I gave the broadcast only half my attention, reserving the other half for the cold, creamy treat I had allowed myself tonight. Then, out of the blue, I heard a familiar name—Carl Hobson. Dozens of reporters were hounding him as he tried to maneuver his way into his D.C. office. I turned up the volume, and set the half-eaten bowl of ice cream on the coffee table.

"Mr. Hobson, how do you respond to the accusations that you deliberately and willfully caused the crash of Flight 9602 last year, killing everyone on board?" one of the reporters grilled him, then jammed a microphone in his face.

"I have no statement at this time," he coldly answered, then disappeared through his office doors.

The cameras returned to the commentators. "There you have it, Joan. That was CIA Director Carl Hobson, who earlier today was accused of planning and carrying out an elaborate plan to assassinate two DEA agents, on their return flight to the United States from Mexico last year. As yet, we don't have all the details. We've been trying to get a comment from the President, but he has not given us any statement."

"Ted, any idea who would have directed Carl Hobson to perform such a barbaric act? Surely he wouldn't have been acting on his own."

"As I said, Joan, we have no details yet. Apparently, a witness turned up with overwhelming evidence to support the accusations against Hobson. There has also been some mention that Claude McCormick, the CEO for Goldbank, is somehow involved. Again, Joan, this is all just speculation. I'm sure things will clear up as we get more information. For now, this is Ted Provost, reporting live from the CIA D.C. headquarters. Back to you, Joan."

The last E-mail document from Hobson to Kephart flashed through my mind. His determination to "take down" everyone he could possibly name, if he were ever in this position, replayed in my head. I wondered how many names he had already sung out.

The next newsclip brought a tear to my eye. The camera crews were camped out on Amanda Powers's front lawn, waiting to get an interview with her. The cameras zoomed in a close-up shot on a little girl peeking out the window of the house. The happy little face with the sparkling eyes I had seen just days before, was now streaked with tears.

Finally, Martha Powers came to the door, and offered a brief statement. "My daughter-in-law has no comment for you right now. Please, leave her alone. She's been through a terrible ordeal. This family needs some peace. Please respect our privacy. Thank you." Then she closed the door.

I felt bad for her, but at least now the truth would come out, and the people responsible would be brought to justice.

The entire news broadcast was devoted to reporting the Hobson incident. Experts predicted indictments would start being handed down as early as next week. A Senate investigation would likely be launched simultaneously. Nothing more was reported about the identity of the witness.

I turned off the TV, and carried my melted bowl of ice cream into the kitchen. I heard a rattling noise coming from the back porch, and went to investigate. I figured it was probably that rascally little raccoon that had decided to set up camp under the back stairs. I had started throwing out scraps of food for him. He became a small nuisance, rattling the garbage cans at night, while I tried to sleep. I peeked out the window of the back door, but didn't see him anywhere. "Hmm . . . he must have heard me coming," I said to myself, as I turned back toward the kitchen.

That's when I saw her. She stood behind the door separating the kitchen from the back porch. Shocked to see her, I started to speak, but a man grabbed me from behind, and put his hand over my mouth.

I recognized Kerstin immediately, but I had no idea who the brute was, dragging me through the house. He shoved me down into a kitchen chair. I wondered if it could be the same man I saw with her in her kitchen that night, in Geneva.

"What are you doing here, Kerstin? What's this all about?" I demanded.

She looked at me, her eyebrows pushing down closer to the bridge of her nose. Those were angry eyes. I'm sure she wondered how I knew who she was. She had no idea I had spied on her. Her hands trembled as she uncoiled a length of cotton rope.

"Oh, I think you know what this is about, Devonie Lace," she replied angrily as she tied my hands and feet to the chair.

"No. I don't know what this is all about. Why in the world did you follow me halfway around the globe? How did you find me?"

"My new friend here, Mr. Khan, has all sorts of resources for finding people," she responded. Her smugness turned my stomach. "Now, where is it?"

"Where is what?"

"Robert's computer. Where is it?" she demanded.

"I don't know what you're talking about. I don't have the computer. It was worthless, so I gave it away," I alleged.

Khan had wandered off into the other room, probably to search for the laptop. I had left it on the desk in the den. It wouldn't be hard to find.

Then, from the other room, he called, "I found it, Kerstin. In here."

She pointed a bony finger at me that translated to "Stay put and shut up . . . or else. . . ."

The two of them argued over who would operate the computer. Finally, I heard her insist she had watched Robert access the account hundreds of times, and she could get it done much faster. Khan gave in to her persistent demands, and stepped aside. She fumbled her way to the

VideoService software, and got connected. The two of them were silent for several minutes. Then the silence was broken, and her rage flew—like that of an angry dog, tormented one too many times.

"What have you done with it!" she screamed, as she ran through the house and back into the kitchen, pointing that finger at me again.

"What have I done with what?" I replied. My calmness infuriated her.

"Why, you little—" she started to say, as she got set to take a swing at me. I closed my eyes, and prepared myself for the blow. Khan entered the room just in time to grab her wrist.

"Wait a minute, Kerstin. Losing control is a sign of poor character. Never lose control," he lectured, as he pulled her away from me.

"She stole our money, and you expect me to stay calm? Robert was right. You are an idiot."

If looks could kill, I'm sure she would have died on the spot. The two of them obviously shared no affection for each other. Their only point of commonality was greed for the money in that bank account.

This time, Khan did the finger-pointing—right in Kerstin's face. "Now, you just sit down there, and keep your mouth shut, woman! I'll take care of this situation from now on. I don't want to hear another word out of you. Understand?" His cold, dark eyes could have belonged to the devil himself.

Instantly, Kerstin shut up. She took tiny steps over to a chair across from me, and melted into it. She laced her fingers together and laid them in her lap, under the table.

"Now, Miss Lace. Why don't you tell me how I can

collect the money owed to me—plus interest—from the bank account you've apparently confiscated.''

"The money is gone. I donated it to the UFO Foundation of the Planet Earth. If you had gotten here yesterday, I could have helped you out. Like they say, timing is everything.''

"That's very funny." He laughed. Then he produced a gun from inside his jacket. He pointed the barrel directly at my head. Beads of sweat formed on his forehead. The smirk left his dark face. "I will ask you again, Miss Lace. This time, you will not disobey me, or I will blow your head off. Understand?" He pronounced each word very deliberately, to assure my comprehension.

Kerstin's eyes grew wide with fear that he would carry out his threat. "Are you crazy? You can't kill her yet—not until we get our hands on that money. She's the only one who can access it.''

"Shut up!" Khan shouted, then turned the gun on her. "I'm sick of listening to your whining voice. It's like fingernails on a chalkboard. One more sound out of you, and I'll put you right out of my misery.''

"So much for maintaining control," she grumbled.

He took aim, one inch to the left of her left ear, and fired his weapon. She didn't say another word. He returned his aim to my head, and asked his question again.

Before I could speak, we were all startled by the crashing sound of breaking glass. Suddenly, there were armed men in black uniforms, with full helmets and bulletproof attire, advancing from all sides. They shouted for Khan to drop his weapon. He maintained his aim on me, as if this would ensure his safety. I held my breath, not knowing just how crazy or desperate this man might be.

Two men, directly behind him, stood like statues, with

their high-powered rifles aimed directly at his head. Another marksman kept his post in the hallway leading from the dining area to the back of the house. One more advanced from the back porch, and drew a bead right between Khan's eyes. The standoff lasted a full two minutes. Sweat poured off Khan's face, like off a blacksmith in the middle of July, working too close to his forge. His hand began to tremble, and I worried he might fire the weapon accidentally—he shook so badly. Finally, he laid down his gun, and gave himself up.

Then two familiar faces entered the kitchen—agents Cooper and Willis from the FBI. I felt like a chicken who had just been rescued from the fox by the coyote.

Kerstin and Khan were handcuffed, and taken away. Cooper untied my hands and feet, and checked to see if I had sustained any wounds.

"We've been chasing you all over the country—all over Europe, too, for that matter. Just what did you think you were doing? Why wouldn't you let us help you?" Cooper demanded as he slammed the ropes down on the table in front of me.

"Why? So you could finish me off, after you missed me the first time on my boat?" I blurted out without thinking.

"What? *Finish you off?* What the heck is that supposed to mean? You think *we* blew up your boat?"

"Darn right, I do. It wasn't until after I came to you that my boat was destroyed, and my friend Jason was almost killed. What was I supposed to think?"

"First of all, we have your friend Jason in protective custody until all the players in this little episode are rounded up and corraled. Second, it wasn't us who blew up your boat, or caused your friend's car accident. You can thank our friend, Mr. Carl Hobson, for that little piece of work.

"Just between you, me, and the fence post, some very wealthy and powerful people donated unbelievable amounts of money to get our current President into the White House. Those people would have been destroyed if the news of their involvement in the Mexican drug cartel got out. Not to mention, several major U.S. banking institutions would likely be crippled if the Mexico-based company couldn't repay its loans. We now believe someone in the White House directed Hobson to have Powers and Norris taken care of—to protect those people. We knew the CIA used Kephart as an asset in other operations involving assassinations of third-world-country military leaders.

"Kephart brought Khan into the picture because of his electronics expertise. We had been looking for Khan for months before you came to us with that device you found. We knew he was one of the few people around who had the expertise to build one. Every time we'd get close to him, or Kephart, Hobson would throw a monkey wrench into our investigation.

"By the time we confirmed what you had brought to us, you had flown yourself halfway around the world. When we tried to bring you in, for your own protection, you led us on some crazy, wild-goose chase. I ought to book you right now and throw you in the slammer, just so we can keep an eye on you until this whole thing is over."

"Then it was Hobson who killed my friend Joe?" I asked.

"No. That credit goes to Mr. Khan, there. Apparently, word got out, in the organized-crime circle, that a friend of Joe's came across Robert Kephart's trademark weapon. Evidently, there was a rather large sum of money owed to

Khan by Kephart. Khan assumed whoever found the gun, probably found the money, too. When Khan confronted Joe, and demanded to know the identity of his friend, Joe refused to tell. So Khan killed him. Bad seed, that Khan is.''

''What's going to happen now?'' I asked.

''Well, no doubt you've seen the news of the Senate investigation. Turns out, Frank Eastwood, one of the FAA investigators, who was presumed dead, has turned up with some very interesting information.''

''Frank Eastwood? So *he's* the chat-room informant. That explains how he knew so much about the crash. What will happen to him? Can you protect him until this is over?''

''We'll do our best. Eastwood doesn't place much trust in the Bureau lately. In fact, we still don't know where he is, exactly. The reporter from the *L.A. Times* has him hidden away somewhere, and won't tell anyone where.''

''How long before we're safe?'' I asked.

''Good question. Could take months, or even longer. Hobson, and some other pretty significant players, are likely going to be indicted. Charges have been filed against people in the CIA, FAA, FBI, and even the White House— and that's just concerning the murder of the two DEA agents. Then there's the whole issue of the Mexican drug cartel being financed by U.S. banks and investors, and that whole conspiracy. It's going to take months to sort through this mess, and until it's all over, I'm not sure you'll be completely safe to walk the streets. I would highly recommend you let us take you into the Witness Protection Program, until this goes to trial.''

''Let me think about it for a while. I need to talk to some people first, before I make a decision.''

"Don't think about it too long, Devonie. In this world, it's a short trip from being safe and sound, in your cozy little boat, floating without a care in the middle of the Pacific, to being fish food for a school of hungry sharks."

"Believe me. I know," I answered. I thought of starting a new life again, just as I had when I bought the *Plan B*. All alone, once more. Safe, with no one to threaten my own little world. I thought of the people who had helped me through this ordeal—Uncle Doug, Aunt Arlene, Jason, and, of course, Craig. I had a lot of thinking to do.

Chapter Twenty-two

It didn't take long to make my decision. I opted for my own witness protection program. It's called *Plan C*—formerly known as *The Jewel*. After making some sizable donations to a few of my favorite charities, I went directly back to Del Mar and bought the sixty-foot luxury sailing yacht, on the spot. Uncle Doug made a very nice commission on the deal. I had a few loose ends to tie up before I could set sail. I bought Jason a new car, since his was destroyed in the accident. Also, I gave him the laptop computer, since I wouldn't have a use for it, sailing around the Caribbean over the next few months. Then there was the small matter of repairs to Doug and Arlene's vacation house in Tahoe. Those FBI guys busted the front door, plus three other windows. What a bunch of animals. But they *did* save my life.

One thing I forgot to consider when I purchased my sixty-foot dream—even with autopilot, it's not quite the same as sailing a little thirty-five-foot sloop around the harbor. I would require a crew to help sail her. How would I find someone who could pick up and leave for several months, to island-hop around the Caribbean? And more important, who could I stand to be around for that length of time, confined to a sixty-foot living area? This would be tougher than I first thought. But, with Uncle Doug's assistance, I put together a crew that's up for the challenge.

So, for my thirty-seventh birthday, here I am, floating somewhere in the middle of the clear blue waters of the Caribbean, sipping on some exotic drink with a pink flower and umbrella sticking out the top. The sun is warm on my bare legs, and the big floppy sun hat I picked up in St. Thomas keeps the sun off my nose. I spent the morning being entertained by a school of porpoises that decided to clown around off the bow of the boat. I haven't read the legal section of a newspaper in weeks, and I haven't looked at a computer in just as many days.

The crew consists of only two people. There's myself, whose duties include cooking, and deciding which island to visit next. I believe that makes me the skipper. Then there's my first mate, who's something of a Jimmy Stewart–type character. He's tall and handsome, and oh yes, he also doubles as the ship's doctor. That would be Craig. He doesn't cook at all, but he always warns me when I'm about to be hit in the head by the boom.

Plan C—I think this may be the best idea I've had yet.